TO: RITA
PEACE ! COLOSSIANS 3:15

GENE

THE MANNY PACQUIAO EFFECT AND OTHER STORIES

Gene P. Del Carmen

ISBN: 1537118439
ISBN 13: 9781537118437

For Raquel and Priscilla

TABLE OF CONTENTS

ACKNOWLEDGMENTS

My sincerest gratitude goes to the people who so kindly and unselfishly shared their time, talents, and constructive comments to help me put this book together.

After writing each story, I always ask my wife, Arielita, to read the first draft. Initially she did not want to read about a story character dying; it somehow upsets her. But part of being a storyteller is having the honesty to tell stories in the manner in which they were meant to be told. If I twist the story towards a happy ending to a tale that isn't supposed to have one, I become unhappy. I thank her for accepting that reality now and telling me constructively what she honestly thinks of them.

I want to thank my nephew, Rey T. Aquino, and his thirteen-year-old daughter, Elizabeth, for their help in editing my stories. Elizabeth is a very good English student in school and is also a budding short-story writer. We have seen her writing and editing talents as she has written short stories for her class. Our writing connection with her that started from my mother, is alive and hopefully will continue to bring a lot more great stories for generations. Elizabeth's father, Rey, was a law student in the Philippines but chose to be a college professor instead. He now works for a big banking institution in Canada.

Another special editor was my good friend from our advertising days, Len Manansala. He helped enhance the narrative for the story "The Manny Pacquiao Effect."

My sister Cristina D. C. Pastor, editor of the online magazine *The Fil-Am*, generously shared her comments and opinions with me when I ask for them.

My valuable story critics were: **Father John Spino**, of Point Pleasant Beach, New Jersey, a semi-retired priest and my very dear friend; my wife's nephew, **Walter O. Espejo** of Nashville, Tennessee, a hardworking father as well as a nurse and realtor; **Nestor J. Tambor,** a retired journalist and businessman, who was a reporter for the Philippine News Service and feature writer for Kislap Graphic Magazine; and my first cousin, **Dr. Alex Del Carmen,** a gifted surgeon and my story critic until he passed away on June 10, 2016. I always mailed the paper manuscripts to his house in Mechanicsburg, Pennsylvania because he preferred that method over e-mail. I pray that his kind soul rests in peace.

I encouraged all my story critics not to hold back and to offer me their frank comments.

I also want to thank my very patient and sometimes blunt story reviewers: **Eduardo Flor** was my high-school classmate at Don Bosco Tech and is now a retired Analyst/Programmer Manager in Fountain Valley, California. **Mary Esther P. Wyman** was my classmate in theology graduate school and is now a retired Directress of Religious Education at St. Joseph's Parish in Tom's River, New Jersey. **Agnes T. Monta** is a registered nurse who manages her husband's medical practice, **Dr. Art. D. Monta,** an internist and nephrologist whose opinion I sought for my story on kidney organ donation, "Solomon, Peter, and Joseph." Both Art and Agnes are very active members of the Catholic family ministry *Bukas Loob sa Diyos* ("Open in Spirit to God") in the Diocese of Trenton, New Jersey. **Lourdes C. Paredes** is a retired registered nurse from Piscataway, New Jersey, who now volunteers in civic and Catholic groups and also loves to travel. And, **Rogie Sanchez**, my longtime friend, is a retiree who is a very eclectic reader.

Also, thanks to my good friend and neighbor, Ned Alesna, a very competent computer expert, who had always helped me with my pc problems sometimes in the middle of writing my manuscripts.

You have all enriched not just my stories but also my otherwise plain and ordinary life. My stories take me to the exciting, challenging, and colorful world of my characters when I write about them and the events that happen to them. With your frank comments, together we engage them, analyze them, and try to lead them, sometimes unsuccessfully, to a much better place.

Thank you all very much.

INTRODUCTION

In my first book, *The Pork Bun Heist and Other Stories,* I wrote of my mother's storytelling talent, which I admit is the enduring connection to my writing today. I got it all from her. When my sister and I were toddlers, our mother, Victoria, would tell us stories, thoughtfully inventing the events as she narrated them to us. The characters and events were so real and alive to me then that there were times when my imagination would recreate the stories and put my own spin on them. It was so much better than being read a bedtime story. She also had a great influence on my life, my morals, and my thoughts. She was able to read and see the stories I wrote for comics and television, but, sadly, neither she nor my father lived long enough to read my first book. I dedicated it to them.

This is my second book of short stories. The title story, "The Manny Pacquiao Effect," was a seed sown after Pacquiao won the match against Oscar De La Hoya. I have become a really big Manny Pacquiao fan since then. There are other short stories in this book about characters and events that I trust you will find fascinating and thought provoking.

I'd like to dedicate this book to two women who were once a big part of my life and continue to be so even after their deaths. As I also mentioned in my first book, my first wife, Raquel San Pedro, passed away due to the kidney ailment called lupus nephritis. Based on my experiences of her sad passing, I have written in this book a true story, "*Solomon, Peter, and Joseph (A True Story)*," that shares some facts about and explores the challenges of kidney donation. I hope all of us will be better informed on this subject, especially the people who are in a position to do something about it. Thirteen kidney patients on the transplant waiting list die every day. We need to do something immediately.

My sister Priscilla Teopisto was eighteen years older than me. Although she grew up with us, she was not my biological sister but my first cousin. My mother and her mother, Teodora, were very dear sisters. Both of Priscilla's parents died during the Japanese occupation of the Philippines. My parents, newly married at that time, offered to take care of her when she was orphaned at the tender age of twelve. Her two other siblings, Patria and Patricio Jr., were embraced by other relatives.

I remember very clearly when I was six years old when she told me she was getting married. She wanted me to be the ring bearer for the wedding ceremony. My initial response to her was "No!" My reason was, I was very shy. She told me we would have a rehearsal before the actual church ceremony and that I was the only one she preferred. She also reminded me that she had frequently changed my diapers when I was a baby. It was one of the early life arguments I lost. We had great fun together as adults.

Although Precy, as she was fondly called, had fallen in love, the marriage did not endure. She managed to finish her college degree in accounting and worked as an accountant for a large pharmaceutical company in Manila. All four of her kids are now married with families of their own.

Priscilla passed away of a brain aneurysm in 2003 at age sixty-nine. My father and I delivered eulogies for her at her funeral service, recalling that smart girl who grew up to be a loving, protective big sister to my sister and I.

As a storyteller, you can see I have a lot of stories to tell from my treasure trove of memories.

THE MANNY PACQUIAO
EFFECT

"Did you tell Rosie you're going to Manila?" There was a note of concern in the voice of Raul's sister, Reny. Her brother was a recently widowed and newly retired Filipino American cardiac surgeon who lived in New Jersey, and he had just decided to devote his retirement to unpaid angioplasties, bypasses, and aneurysm repairs in the ghetto.

"No, I didn't tell any of our relatives," Raul replied calmly to appease his sister's apprehension as they sipped mimosas. The poolside cabana at Reny's house on Long Island, New York, was a pleasant setting for the siblings' farewell chat. His half-closed eyes made a sweep of the upscale fineries that never seemed to erase Reny's Manila accent.

"I don't want them to throw parties for me," Raul added, with images flashing through his mind of being fixed up with aging town beauties and newly minted widows. "I'll let them know when I'm settled in my condo."

"I can't help but worry about you and your fresh single life in Manila," Reny teasingly insisted on counseling her brother. "You're a heart surgeon; a handsome doctor like you is a big, easy target. You might as well pin a sign on your back that says, 'Marry me. I'm a rich American doctor.'"

Raul was a slim, muscular, lifelong jogger, gifted with genes from generations that subsisted on sweet-potato tops, fish heads, unpolished rice, and the Filipino 110-proof version of Kickapoo Joy Juice from coconuts. Raul was not exactly a looker, but his aura of a primitive brown idol often turned the heads of nurses and patients' visitors. Dr. Raul, as he was fondly called, had been the director of the cardiac-surgery department at the New Jersey hospital where he'd worked for twenty-six years. His wife, Tess, had passed away two years ago, just as they were planning their retirement. With three grown children on their own, he had been persuaded by a college classmate, Dr. Sid, the dean of the college of medicine at their old university, to come to Manila to perform pro bono heart surgery for slum dwellers, and indigents in Manila and possibly in far-flung towns who could ill afford a checkup, much less an open-heart operation. His surgeon's hands were still firm and sure, Raul had thought. The kids were on their own, and his finances were secure. Heck, he could afford to do it.

Brother and sister stayed silent, mimosas in hand, as they watched the big red sun come down over the cabana's roof.

"Tell me," Reny said over the rim of her cocktail glass, "however did Dr. Sid manage to twist your arm to give up a blissful retirement for the underbelly of Mom's beloved hometown?"

"Yes," Raul replied, "Sid kept bugging me to practice altruism while we still can, to not leave a bequest for charity after we choked. And here's what he said that really hit me. He said to give as much as you take, just like Manny Pacquiao." The Filipino boxing icon was the best pound-for-pound fighter in the world.

"But Manny Pacquiao is an elected politician," Reny replied cynically. "He has to operate on altruism. He can afford it too."

"Well, Sid is right," Raul said, slowly standing from the lounge chair and viewing the sun's magic-mirror descent through his glass. "Filipinos in America have been truly blessed; we must give some of those blessings back to the poor in our country." He paused. "Remember when Sid and I went to Las Vegas to see Pacquiao's fight with Oscar De La Hoya at the MGM Grand?" And had any Filipino not watched? Forty million pairs of eyes from every nook of the more than seven thousand islands making up the Philippine archipelago had been glued to the TV as the soft-spoken Filipino had beaten the golden boy of boxing.

"As MGM Grand high rollers, Sid and I were among the lucky ones to be invited to Manny's party after the fight," Raul continued, eyes glazing over with the memory. "That's when Manny Pacquiao advised us to help the poor in our country. I will never forget that moment; he was very sincere. At that time of his greatest triumph, Pacquiao could have told us to donate our hearts and livers to the needy and we would have done it without a second thought."

Raul took a quick sip of his mimosa and then continued. "I really did not need much convincing, not from Pacquiao or Sid or anyone else. I wanted to do it, and I want to even more so now that Tess has passed away." Reny could see that her brother's mind was made up. Looking at the pensive Raul with newfound admiration, Reny went back to a subject of more pressing concern.

"How about Rosie, our ever-dependent half-sister?" she asked. Raul was visibly upset out of his boxing-idol reverie. He began having flashes of birthday parties missed by their father and of dolls, carelessly hidden in drawers, with a strange girl's name on the gift wrap. Echoes of their mother's cries of deep anguish over the affair now rang in Raul's ears.

Reeling from the vision of their mother's unhappy death, Raul walked toward his sister. "I heard that Rosie's deep into drugs now," he said, "so that's why I didn't tell our relatives I was coming." Raul shook his head in exasperation, the kind that anyone feels when the name of a family's black sheep intrudes into pleasant conversation.

Rosie was their father's love child with his on-and-off mistress. Their father had been a lawyer who had worked as a government bureaucrat and been known as the straightest of arrows. Perhaps that's why the discovery of his infidelity had been all the more jarring for everyone, especially his wife and children.

Their mother had been a stern schoolteacher who had cared devotedly for them and inspired them to excel in school. Growing up in a suburb of Manila, Raul and Reny had been bright, motivated students, thanks to the loving guidance of their mother. They had been academically gifted and were relentlessly boosted by motherly love and near-adulation of their successful father. Eventually, Raul had become a doctor and Reny an economist, achievements their parents had been so proud of.

But even the glossiest marble floor hides a crack somewhere. When the siblings were in their early college years, they had discovered that the father they worshipped had a secret second family he kept at the far edge of their hometown. From snatches of malicious gossip posing as neighborly concern, they had learned that their father's mistress was a shapely, much younger waitress at a watering hole frequented by bureaucrats. Raul and Reny were the last ones to know. They later found out that there had been a baby girl born out of the affair. When she'd been baptized, the clandestine lovers had named her Rosie, a name starting with the letter *R*, just like their father's name and each of theirs.

Their mother had played the martyr, silently suffering the betrayal, smiling bravely, and keeping up the front of the dutiful wife. This masquerade was carried on for years. Not a word disparaging their father was ever heard in the house.

Rosie grew up without the warm but strict guidance from her father's legal wife. It was that kind of guidance that nurtured Raul and Reny and enabled them to blossom into ambitious achievers. Emotionally battered by her husband's betrayal, Raul and Reny's mother devoted her life to her children's education until their ultimate triumph as young professionals in New York.

"Did you know that I spoke to Rosie on the phone about three months ago?" Reny admitted. "She said her daughter is now a teenager. Rosie wanted to buy her a nice dress for her birthday."

"Did you send her money?" Raul asked.

"How could I not? She started crying on the phone again, playing her guilt-trip act to the hilt. You know how she always does that, as if we owe her a living for being the 'other' child."

Then Reny had to stop the unpleasant subject. She intended to send her brother off not with a heavy load but with an airy lift. "Did you say you will also be teaching cardiac surgery at the university?" Reny shifted the topic blithely.

"Yes, and I'll schedule surgery for the indigents at the hospital on days that I'm not teaching."

Reny gazed at her brother's bronzed, middle-aged face in admiration. "You really like being a doctor, huh?"

"It's all I ever wanted to be. You know that," Raul said, reminiscing.

"Too bad none of your children became doctors."

"Well, Tess and I encouraged them to be doctors, but none of them wanted to," Raul answered, shaking his head. "I guess my umbilical cord didn't connect well with them," Raul added.

"They do have your drive and ambition, though, and they're all doing well. That's enough umbilical cord connection right there." Brother and sister both laughed, and Reny felt nostalgic after that.

"I wish I could go with you," she said as she smiled. "I miss those big, sweet carabao mangoes." Her mouth watered at the thought.

"You can visit me anytime," Raul graciously offered, "and I'll make sure to have the sweetest and juiciest carabao mangoes laid out on the table for you. You can have all the mangoes you want."

Reny hugged her older brother tightly and whispered in his ear, "I'm proud of you, Kuya" ["older brother"]. "But stay away from those pretty interns." They laughed softly behind affectionate tears.

As the Philippine Airlines plane descended, Raul saw the streets of Manila below already starting to get crammed with traffic, signaling a busy workday. The jet touched down with a smooth landing, as Raul had expected, at Manila's Ninoy Aquino International Airport at five thirty in the morning. He said a short prayer of thanks and then got up and proceeded to customs inspection. He was standing by a luggage carousel that was three-deep with disembarked passengers when he felt a tap on his right shoulder.

"Dr. Raul Gomez?" It was a polite male airport employee. He was wearing a white, short-sleeved shirt with black shoulder bars.

"Yes!" Raul fairly jumped.

"There is someone waiting for you at the exit gate." The official-looking man picked up his two pieces of luggage, turned, and walked briskly away with Raul tailing him. It happened so fast that Raul did not even have a chance to ask how this official-looking guy knew his name.

But instead of leading Raul to the clearly marked exit gate, where he saw people waiting for arrivals from New York, Raul's escort made a sharp left to a side door, at which another local man in a white T-shirt greeted him. The man looked tired and not so clean.

"Good morning, Dr. Gomez. I will take you to your condo," the new escort greeted him in a bored tone.

"*Now, who the heck is this guy?*" Raul wondered to himself. "*Oh, perhaps* Reny e-*mailed relatives anyway and asked them to send somebody*," Raul thought. "*What a sis, that Reny!*" He visibly relaxed at the comforting thought.

The bored-faced man in the white T-shirt opened the trunk of an old blue Toyota Corolla and dumped the luggage there. Raul, being tired, settled in the backseat. The man in the white T-shirt sat in the front passenger seat and snapped at the driver, "*Tira!* Let's go!"

The car traveled at whiplash speed. The driver knew the way very well, avoiding traffic lights and missing indifferent passengers by a hair. The sun was starting to come up when Raul felt the hair on the back of his neck stand on end. Could these two guys really be the right people to pick him up and take him to his condo? Who were these bozos?

"Hey, where exactly are you taking me?" he asked nervously in his stammering Tagalog. He continued, yelling, "Who are you, anyway?" Instead of responding, the man in the white T-shirt pulled out a nasty-looking .22-caliber revolver and pointed it at Raul's face.

"Stay down!" the armed thug hissed. "Lie on the seat and be quiet, or I'll kill you!"

Raul did as he was told, realizing what was happening to him. He was being kidnapped. Raul closed his eyes and silently prayed. "God, what did I get myself into? Please don't let them kill me, God. My kids need me, my sister needs me, and my patients need me. God, I pray for these two guys who have abducted me; please, God, make them realize the wrong they have done. I am here to help my people in your name and to glorify you!" He prayed desperately, mouthing the words in between sobs.

Then he remembered Manny Pacquiao. Yes, the most recognizable and revered name among close to one hundred million Filipinos all over the world. Manny Pacquiao. The Pac-Man. A plan quickly lighted on his brain, and he prayed so hard that the plan he was feverishly hatching would work. Still crouched in the back seat, Raul opened his eyes. He pulled out his cell phone. Steadying his nerves, and with the loudest voice of authority he could muster, Raul yelled, "Hey! I am the personal doctor of Manny Pacquiao! Do you hear me? I am Pac-Man's doctor! Here, you can see my picture with Manny Pacquiao on my cell phone!" Raul pulled out his cell phone and swiped the screen, scrolling wildly to get to the photo.

Clearly intrigued, the man in the white T-shirt turned to the still-crouching Raul, grabbed the cell phone, and touched the screen to see the picture. And there it was, a selfie of the famed boxer-politician, flanked by Raul and Dr. Sid and surrounded by delirious fans, the trainer Freddie Roach, and assorted groupies at the MGM Grand.

"I'm supposed to see him at Sarangani (Pacquiao's home province) on Friday," Raul shouted. He tried to steady his nervous breathing. "If I don't show up, Pacquiao's people and the entire Philippine army will be hunting for you two!" Raul spoke with growing confidence in his voice, which seemed to make the kidnappers stop and think.

After driving for another ten minutes across slums and streets in a car with no name plates, they made a full stop at a remote edge of what appeared to be an enormous garbage dump. Raul could smell the intense stench, the methane fuming from the decaying mounds of waste. He realized that if these two guys wanted to kill him, this was the place to do it. They could simply dump his body here, where it would rot and end up as an unrecognizable heap. Again, Raul tried to reason with his tormentors.

"Look, guys, I realize you want money from me. You can't get any ransom money from me, you know! I'm a single man; my wife died two years ago. I have no one. I retired from the hospital, so they have no attachments to me. They won't care if you kill me. Nobody will pay ransom!"

"Shut up!" the man in the white T-shirt growled, with some visible doubt on his knotted forehead.

"Please don't kill me, because you'll end up with nothing!" Raul pleaded again. "I have about eight hundred dollars in my wallet. You can take that," he said, reaching for his back pocket. "I also have a gold chain. Take it too!" With his hands shaking, he showed them the gold chain still hanging from his neck.

The two kidnappers got out of the car and talked outside in muffled, hurried tones. Raul could hear them engaging in a heated argument. After about five minutes, the man in the white T-shirt opened the back door and roughly pulled Raul out by the collar. Raul caught a sickening whiff of ammonia from the man's armpits.

"Okay, doctor, hand over your wallet!" the man said. Raul carefully did as he was told. The man in the white T-shirt took out the thick wad of dollar bills and Raul's credit cards and then gave the now-empty wallet back to him.

"Now, take off your shirt and shoes!" the man commanded. Raul was wearing a Ralph Lauren cotton shirt with the unmistakable Polo logo. His shoes were light-brown Nike sneakers with dark brown stripes, easily worth fifty dollars to the trained eye of a thief. As Raul undressed, the man took off his white T-shirt and shoes. They traded clothes and sneakers, since Raul and the duo's apparent leader were about the same size.

"The gold chain too!" the man demanded. Raul raised the chain over his head to take it off. He gave it to the man, who was now wearing his Polo shirt. Raul's wedding ring gleamed in the early sunlight. Judging from his look, the man appeared to want that prize.

"Please don't take my wedding ring. That is the only memory I have of my late wife," Raul begged.

The man in the Polo shirt reached for Raul's wrist and forced the ring from Raul's finger, leaving a gash. Quickly examining the ring for apparent value, the man saw the name Tess engraved on the back. He gazed quizzically at Raul, who was by then shamelessly whimpering. To Raul's amazement, the ring was shoved back into his face. The other man got back inside the car and started it. The man in the Polo shirt then got into the passenger seat and shut the door.

"Okay, doctor, we're leaving you; you're on your own," Raul heard the man bark in his ear. "The main road is not far from here. Don't make the mistake of reporting this to the police, or I will go after you, break your face, and kill you like a rat!" The voice was loud and threatening. Raul's tormentor, clad in expensive, stateside clothes for probably the first time, now felt empowered to snarl unreasonable commands at this pathetic, rich American boy wearing a sweaty, torn T-shirt and muddy sneakers. Raul nodded helplessly in agreement.

When the car left, Raul closed his eyes and heaved a deep sigh of relief. *He was alive.* He came so close to being dead, a nameless carcass in a dump site. But he was alive. Again he prayed to God in thanks for his apparent resurrection. He walked about half a mile and then flagged an empty taxicab that took him back to the airport. He found a pale and worried Dr. Sid and the police waiting for him.

"Raul, I was here waiting for you when your flight landed. What happened to you?" Dr. Sid asked, looking aghast at his bedraggled friend, whose face was still streaked with tears. Raul told them his kidnapping story. After he gave his statement to the police, the two doctors went to the airport restaurant. Raul was extremely hungry, and his limbs were visibly shaking from the harrowing ordeal. His first bites of rice and pork adobo calmed his edgy nerves and filled his empty stomach. He was lucky to be alive.

"So, Manny Pacquiao saved your life, huh, Raul?" Dr. Sid asked incredulously.

"I know it sounds straight out of a movie," Raul replied in between grateful gulps. "But I showed them our selfie with Pac-Man right after the De La Hoya bout, and it worked. Pacquiao is much more intriguing than I thought. Almost mystical, you know?

And those are not just the delusions of a man who just got a new lease on life. Those two kidnappers really came to their senses. I tell you, the very mention of Pacquiao's name jarred them." To satisfy Dr. Sid's curiosity, Raul reached for his back pocket and felt for his cell phone. Just then he realized that the kidnappers had taken it too.

"That was very smart thinking, Raul," said Dr. Sid in admiration. "I don't know if I could ever think that way and that quickly in a similar situation."

"Not my time to die," Raul said, smiling. But then he was suddenly curious.

"Sid, did you tell anybody that I was coming?"

"Well, my staff and I knew but nobody else."

After the two friends left the airport restaurant, Raul could think of only one place that he wanted to visit next, soiled T-shirt and all. "Sid, I'd like to go to Baclaran Church. That's about fifteen minutes from the airport."

"After all those decades in the United States? You must be a devotee."

"My mother was," Raul explained. "She always took my sister and I to Baclaran every Wednesday for the novena."

Baclaran Church had been run by the Redemptorist priests since 1866. With its Romanesque architecture, it was one of the largest Roman Catholic churches not only in the Philippines but in all of Asia. It was home of the Mother of Perpetual Help novena, which was instituted in 1906. Millions of devotees flock to this church for the Wednesday novenas to seek healing, improve fortunes, and lighten their life burdens.

"The church hasn't changed much," Raul observed, taking in its facade with a long, sweeping gaze. It was four o'clock on a Monday afternoon, and the pews were mostly empty but for a few stragglers, older women, and beggars. He remembered the ornate marble altar, the wooden pews, and the familiar church grounds that were filled with devotees every Wednesday for the novenas. Across the street from the church were the shops and restaurants where his mother would take them for a treat after the service. Except for the new fast-food chains like McDonalds and Chow-King, he had intimated to Dr. Sid, the area looked much the same as his last visit ages ago.

Raul knelt intently and bowed his head in prayer while his friend sat in the pew eyeing him with far-reaching understanding. He knew that Raul was filled with immeasurable gratitude after that stressful kidnapping experience. Dr. Sid knelt next to his good friend and said a prayer of gratitude himself. After about fifteen minutes, Raul lifted his head and opened his eyes. He was in tears. Dr. Sid offered his handkerchief. As Raul wiped his eyes dry, he saw a familiar face out of the corner of one of them.

"Sid, that's the guy who kidnapped me!" Raul pointed to a younger man coming down from the choir-loft stairs. Incredibly, he looked just like Raul's kidnapper; this serene-looking man from the choir section was a duplicate of the gruff man in the white T-shirt with an angular face. At that electric moment, Raul could have felled his friend with a nudge.

"Wait, Raul," Dr. Sid cautioned as his friend appeared to be moving toward the look-alike. "I don't think we should confront him; you said he had a gun!"

The younger man was now walking toward them with what seemed like an otherworldly air. He was wearing a clean and crisp white long-sleeved shirt, blue dress pants, and shiny leather shoes. Unlike the kidnapper, he was clean shaven and had a beatific smile on his face. He smiled at the two doctors as he passed and bowed his head slightly in apparent respect to the strangers. Raul could no longer help himself.

"Hey, wait, mister!" Raul yelled, shattering the tranquil air of the church. The man turned around and calmly walked toward the two uneasy doctors.

"Yes, sir, may I help you?" came the soft reply. The man's strangely angelic smile was unmoved.

"Didn't you kidnap me earlier today and rob me of my money and valuables?" Raul was now shaking from head to toe. He was subconsciously drawing courage from the presence of Sid.

The young man could see the anxiety on the doctors' faces. He also recognized the dirty clothes Raul was wearing. He knew right away.

Somewhere in the cosmic scheme of things, and contrary to Albert Einstein's musings, God does play dice with the lives of men and women. Human entanglements are rooted in unimagined probabilities. Miracles do happen, not only in the minds of people of faith but also in the cynical eyes of people of science, for whom guardian angels work wonders in the comforting guise of coincidence.

"I have a twin brother. His name is Berto, and God knows he is always in trouble with the law," the man told the two doctors as he guided them back to their pew. "I heard that Berto was recently paroled from jail." Noticing the consternation of Raul and Dr. Sid, he continued sympathetically. "Why? Did Berto do something bad to you?" He knew that any mention of his twin brother's name was nearly always followed with a word like *theft, assault,* or *violence.*

"Yes! Earlier today, he kidnapped me!" Raul said angrily.

"I am so sorry, sir! My name is Ben, and I am the church organist. I don't even know where my brother Berto is, but I can tell you where he usually hangs out so you can inform the police." Ben was evidently trying to be helpful; he wanted to right the wrong his twin brother had committed. After the initial shock of that confrontation that still echoed in the silence of the surroundings, the three men sat on the pews, and Ben started to explain.

"I am a computer engineer," he began. "I come to Baclaran on Monday afternoons to practice my music on the church organ, and I rehearse with the choir in the evening. I also play at the Savoy Hotel piano bar two nights a week." From Ben's saintly demeanor and gentle voice, Raul gradually became convinced that he was not his former captor, but Raul had to blurt out what was troubling him at that moment.

"I have a disturbing feeling that your brother knew I was coming from the States. I was not a random pick; I could tell he was waiting for me." Raul's mind was now racing with how to fit these puzzle pieces into a grand, orchestrated scheme.

"As I said, Dr. Gomez," Ben replied, "I haven't seen my brother in a while. I have bailed him out of a lot of bad situations before. I can't and I don't want to have anything to do with Berto anymore." Ben raised his hands in surrender. Raul had by then calmed down as he and Dr. Sid continued the furtive conversation.

"We believe you, Ben, but we need to keep Dr. Gomez here safe and with no more threats to his life," Dr. Sid contributed.

"What I'll do for you is go to the police precinct and tell them where Berto might be found. I don't mind doing that. People are safer and Manila is a better place when he is locked up," Ben replied with conviction. And then, as if rousing himself from a bad dream, he abruptly changed the subject, a new gleam in his eye.

"I can't help but feel guilty about Dr. Raul's mishap with Berto," he admitted, seeing that the doctors were getting up from their pew.

"No, please, don't be," the two doctors blurted out at the same time.

"Anyway, you can lighten my load if you join me at the Savoy Hotel tomorrow night for dinner. It's the least I can do," Ben said amiably. Food always seemed to be a comforting salve for a festering wound, a corrector of negative situations.

"We'll be there!" Dr. Sid quickly accepted the invitation, touched by the gesture of kindness from their new friend. The three shook hands in relief, happy to break the ice after the awkward start. But Raul had a last-minute question. There was a nagging thought in his mind.

"Ben, do you know whether Berto has a wife or girlfriend?" Raul asked.

"Yes," Ben quickly replied. "Berto has been with this woman who is older than he is. Sadly, she is also a drug addict."

"Do you happen to know her name?"

"Her name is Rosie."

That night, at his condo in the financial district of Makati City, Raul called Reny and told her everything that had happened on his first day in Manila, including the unlikely connection with their half-sister. Reny was furious and approaching hysteria, not only distraught about her brother's near-death mishap but also raving mad at what she sensed was Rosie's part in the kidnapping.

"The ingratitude of that woman! It would not be beneath Rosie to come at you again through her criminal ties," she warned.

"Don't worry, Ren, I'll be okay!" he said. But Raul was not totally sure.

The moon was full that Tuesday evening as seen over Manila Bay across the street from the Savoy Hotel. Raul recalled the last beautiful golden sunset he had shared in New York with his sister. But this glorious Manila sunset, one of which had dazzled General Douglas MacArthur in his suite at the Manila Hotel ages ago, was one of the most spectacular he had ever seen. It was at once topaz bordering on aquamarine, flecked with feathery gold, a miracle that not even a million scientists and the brainiest of brain surgeons could hope to conjure in their lifetimes.

There was a steady stream of guests, dressed in casual Manila freshness. The men at the hotel wore light, well-tailored blazers over button-down shirts, which was what the two doctors wore as well. The friends had arrived after an exhausting ten-hour stretch at the hospital and were ready for a good

Filipino dinner and some light music. They soon spotted Ben caressing the keys of his baby-grand piano, updating with a touch of jazz an old Filipino love song that some Caucasian guests were trying rather comically to sing together. They were happily mangling the Tagalog vowels. Ben graciously joined them in three-part harmony, his tinkling piano keys nudging the guests back in tune and in tempo. Ben saw the two doctors approaching and waved them to the piano.

"I'll be taking a break in a few minutes. Go get your drinks at the bar, and we'll have dinner together."

Raul and Dr. Sid nursed their San Miguel beers at the bar as they reviewed the events of the past two days.

"Exciting enough for you, Raul?" Dr. Sid jested.

"Too much excitement for my taste, Sid!" Raul answered. Then he asked his longtime friend, "What do you think of our new friend Ben?"

"He seems real and sincere, hardworking, and clearly blessed with talent. And he volunteers his time and musical skills at Baclaran Church. What a guy!" Dr. Sid replied.

"Doesn't he remind you even just a little of our buddy Manny Pacquiao?"

Dr. Sid thoughtfully sipped his beer, saying, "You know, altruism comes in many forms, my friend. Some acts of kindness are random and evidently heartfelt, such as the ones that Pac-Man is often associated with. At the same time, a few acts of generosity may be imposed on the rich and famous because of social expectations."

"What are you saying?" asked Raul.

Before Dr. Sid could respond, Ben tapped them each on the shoulder from behind, and the reverie over Manny Pacquiao was broken. The three sauntered toward the dining room that specialized in Filipino fusion cuisine. Ben led them to a table by the window. To Raul and Dr. Sid's surprise, a teenage girl was sitting at the table, evidently waiting for them. Ben introduced her.

"This is my niece, Blanca. She is joining us for dinner."

Raul stared quizzically at the teenager's regular and unblemished features. He felt queasy. The girl bore a discomfiting resemblance to a scarred face that had menaced Raul's dreams these past few nights.

"Blanca is the daughter of Berto and Rosie," Ben said.

Quite taken aback, the two doctors managed to stutter their hellos, avoiding Blanca's eyes. Ben ignored their discomfort and went ahead with the introductions, aware of the awkwardness in the air.

"Blanca, these two men are Dr. Raul Gomez and Dr. Sid," Ben explained. He paused and then continued, saying, "Dr. Raul is your uncle. He is the half-brother of your mother."

Raul felt that if he didn't say something mundane, his head would explode. "Well, hello! Hi, uh, Blanca. How old are you, child?" Raul asked the fidgeting girl, extending his hand. Dr. Sid reached out his hand also.

"Twelve, po." Blanca addressed Raul using the Tagalog term reserved to show respect for older people and figures of authority.

"I did not know I would meet you tonight; I am so happy to see you, Blanca!" Raul kept the frozen, astonished look on his face. He was finally meeting his niece, who, before now, had been only a name in passing between him and Reny. His eyes were transfixed on the comely teenager. His own flesh and blood, Raul gasped to himself. He felt a lump in his throat, irritated at his own undefined emotions.

"I am also happy to see you, Tito (*uncle*)!" Blanca replied. "I have heard my mother talk about you and Tita (*aunt*) Reny in America." Her eyes gleamed and she smiled humbly as she uttered the words. She was awestruck at seeing this distinguished-looking doctor, her relative, from America.

They all sat down at the table. The two doctors were astounded at the smart and disarmingly frank girl carefully unfolding her napkin and gently laying it on her lap. She kept her unblinking eyes fixed on Raul. Ben was quick to explain.

"Blanca is a very bright girl," he said with obvious pride. Blanca and Ben shared such a look of uncanny but beguiling serenity that Raul felt his face go steaming hot. He was totally befuddled at the fast-evolving events.

"Indeed?" was all that Raul could extract from his parched mouth. "Well, how bright are you, Blanca?" He felt a torrent of intimate questions welling up in his chest, but he decided that asking at a gradual pace was more appropriate. After all, they were practically strangers. But Blanca showed no signs of timidity.

"I have been an honor student since grade one," Blanca answered matter-of-factly but not without modesty. Blanca bowed her head politely to Raul to acknowledge their newfound ties.

There was one question Raul had to ask, and if he had to wait any longer, he would burst. "Tell me, Blanca, how is your mother?" he said. Now that he had met Blanca, he wanted to know more about his other sister.

"I don't know, Tito. My parents have not visited me for about a year." She looked at Raul with abruptly saddened eyes and then continued to nibble on her rice and mini eggrolls in silence.

"As I told you before, we have not seen them for a while," Ben said. Then he changed the subject. Suspecting that his two new friends were hesitant to ask, he made clear why Blanca was there at the hotel, the only child in a vast, buzzing, and adult-smelling room.

"Blanca likes coming here with me to the hotel when I work at the piano bar. The hotel gives me a free room. She does her homework there while I work. It's air-conditioned, you see. She already knows all the hotel employees by name."

"Small wonder why you're always an honor student!" Dr. Sid remarked at the teenager, who seemed too inspired to blush.

"I like the desserts here too!" Blanca remarked, and Raul noticed her digging into her mango ice cream. An inexplicable warm glow was slowly engulfing him.

"You know, Blanca," said Raul tenderly, "your Tita Reny is crazy about mango ice cream, just like you." Blanca smiled at this new uncle from America and nodded happily at discovering a shared family quirk.

Raul could not stop staring at the girl. He was totally disarmed. Feeling a rush of near-filial pride, he followed up with what seemed like a mundane question. "What do you want to be when you grow up, Blanca?"

Blanca stopped eating her ice cream, looked at Raul, and replied politely, "I want to be a doctor, Tito." Raul was visibly moved by his niece's early, confidently stated ambition. He asked, "Why do you want to be a doctor, my child?"

"I want to help people," she replied artlessly, still meeting Raul's gaze as she calmly continued to eat her ice cream.

She's so sure of being a doctor; she's so self-aware and has no second thoughts at all, Raul mused to himself, not without a little regret about his grown-up children in the States, all of whom were nauseated by the mere mention of blood. Another doctor in the family, he thought. Another altruistic dreamer. How about that!

Raul and Sid brimmed with a lot more questions for Blanca, all of which the girl responded to with naive but unmistakable cleverness. After about half an hour, Ben looked at his watch. His dinner break was about to end, so he turned to Blanca and said, "When you finish your ice cream, Blanca, please go up to the room and finish your homework, okay?" Blanca obediently finished the last licks of her ice cream. To Raul, the girl could not have been more different from the jaded kids in American suburbia whose parents could never seem to please them.

"I'm finished, po!" Blanca asked to be excused. She got up from the table and politely bowed to the two doctors. She appeared to be a happy child despite her difficult situation—perpetually smiling, always respectful, clever, but never too forward when speaking.

But then something clouded her joyful demeanor. Instead of heading out of the restaurant, Blanca stiffened and bit her lower lip. It appeared that it was now her turn to talk to the doctors on her own terms. She made a quick respectful glance at Ben, then spoke and unloaded her heavy heart to Raul.

"Tito Raul, I know I have no right to ask you for a favor since we've just met," the girl said in an even tone, sounding much older than her age. "But please help my father and mother. They have been in and out of rehab." Her face became shadowed with gloom. "They cannot recover from their drug addiction, no matter how much I pray for them. And I have prayed and prayed and prayed!" Tears now welled in Blanca's eyes.

His heart breaking, Raul stifled a moan and bent to embrace Blanca as her thin chest heaved with sobs.

"I will surely help them, Blanca. I think that's another reason why I had to come home." Raul patted her head reassuringly. Dr. Sid was also touched by her plea for help. He added, "Yes, Blanca, we have a good rehab facility in Alabang. As long as your mom and dad are willing to get help, your Tito Raul and I will definitely help them; we promise you."

Beaming with the promise of hope, she stood up straight to thank the two doctors. She began by thanking them in Tagalog. "Maraming salamat po. Good night, Tito Raul. Good night Dr. Sid!"

Raul leaned over and again enveloped his niece tightly in his arms; he wished he could talk to her some more. Blanca twisted herself free from Raul's arms and walked toward the elevators. She looked back at Raul, who was still marveling at her tiny figure, and then made the right turn to the elevators.

Raul could not contain his curiosity at the surprising, quickly moving events.

"I can't believe Rosie has not visited her daughter for that long. Where is she now?" Raul asked, turning to Ben.

"We don't know; they don't have a permanent address," Ben replied.

"Is that why Blanca is living with you, Ben?"

"Yes. My wife and I have raised her since she was a baby," Ben explained further. "We enrolled her in a private school because wasting her many talents would have made the tragedy of her life a lot worse." Raul felt a lightness in his chest all at once, as if a long-suppressed breath had escaped.

"This is quite a discovery," Raul said, unable to contain his excitement. "I didn't know I had a bright, gifted niece waiting for me here. What a life-changing discovery! I bet Ren will fall off her chair when she hears this!"

"And Blanca wants to be a doctor too, Raul!" Dr. Sid chimed in.

"Yes, can you believe that kid?"

"Believe? Just picture her walking the halls of our college of medicine!" Dr. Sid beamed.

Raul had to ask. "Do you have other children, Ben?"

"I have a seventeen-month-old son, Ben Jr. My wife is with him now." The three men chatted briefly about their family lives until it was time for Ben to resume his stint at the piano bar.

It had been a chaotic two days for Raul, an emotional roller coaster with ups just as heady as the downs. The discovery of his niece had upended the bizarre, frightening kidnapping that had rudely welcomed him home to Manila. He was suddenly overwhelmed with conflicting emotions, which were energizing and numbing at the same time. On the ride home, Raul was quiet. He felt a tear roll down his cheeks, but he had a smile on his face. Then he realized that Dr. Sid was oddly twisting in his seat and was eyeing him with an expression he couldn't place.

"What's on your mind, Sid?"

"I have to be honest with you, Raul," Sid confessed. He knew that now was the time to own up. "You wondered how Rosie knew about your arrival at the airport. It was me. I was the one who told Rosie your flight schedule."

"What? Why...how," Raul stammered, "how did she convince you?"

"Forgive me, my friend, and believe that I had no choice. Rosie told me that you were her half-brother. She cried hysterically on the phone when I refused to give her the information. What could I do?"

"Rosie does that all the time when she calls us asking for money," Raul said limply.

"And she never told you she had a daughter?"

"Oh, we knew. In fact, she used Blanca to get money from Reny and me."

The car drove smoothly through Manila's late-evening traffic. The multicolored passenger jeepneys hurried about in all directions, cutting each other off in a rush to get the remaining evening fares. Some neon signs started to dim and gradually darken. There was a quiet, uneasy break in their conversation. Dr. Sid noticed more tears welling up in Raul's eyes before he quickly wiped them away with the back of his hand. The tears held the sustained smile on his lips.

"What are you thinking, Raul?" Dr. Sid asked.

Raul took a deep breath as he shook his head, seemingly dazed at the unexpected personal connection he had just established. An image flashed before him, a piece of anatomy that he had seen hundreds of times at the hospital. "Umbilical cord, Sid!" he declared.

"Umbilical cord what?"

"I just found the connection to my umbilical cord, Sid!" Raul's tears kept flowing, and he kept wiping them. Sid could only smile at his friend's overwhelming joy at this discovery.

"Blanca is at the other end of my umbilical cord, Sid. Don't you see? It's not Rosie! Sure, Blanca's mother and I share genes from our father, but we were never joined at the navel." Raul's words gushed out like a relentless torrent, snarled and tripped by the tears and by the saliva from his twitching mouth. "The dirty secret that our relatives were snickering

about behind our backs, yes. Our mother's toxic ha-
tred that she took to her grave—that's it. Our bitter
envy and resentment for the years that our father
showered on our other sister! Those umbilical cords
were never joined, Sid. We never accepted our father's cruelty or his emotional abandonment."

Raul paused, the snot from his nose dripping to
his knee. "Sid, Blanca—my niece—this incredible
girl, wants to be a doctor. Don't you see that Rosie
and Berto were not able to poison her with their
blood? Blanca is the fleshy lifeline that has reached
out to me from the navel of my soul, not from the
cord that sustained her in Rosie's womb. Sid, I will
do everything, everything, Sid, my friend, and you've
got to help me, to make her dream come true." Raul
was ecstatic. Tremors shook his entire body, and his
whole shirt was damp with sweat.

After a minute or two, after Raul appeared to
have come down from the heights of self-discovery,
Sid joked lightly, "Aren't you glad I convinced you to
come home?"

"Yes, I am thankful for more than you can ever
know," Raul murmured. "I knew there was a reason
why I was led to come home to Manila, Sid." He
paused to take a deep breath and then excitedly continued to fit the puzzle pieces together. "Imagine,
Sid, if I had not been kidnapped by Blanca's father.
I would not have picked out Ben at Baclaran Church
and would not have been led to Blanca."

"Things really do happen for a reason; I witnessed that just now," Sid replied softly.

"You know, Sid, I had to defend altruism to Reny when I decided to accept your job offer. She was skeptical whether it was right for me." He paused and then bolted upright as if electrified. "She doubted Manny Pacquiao's motives for giving away millions to our country's poor, who could turn their backs on him when he is no longer rich and famous."

Raul, visibly shaken, turned slowly to Sid. "Sid, Manny Pacquiao is right; altruism brings natural joy to one's whole being, because you know what? Giving selflessly and of himself is Manny's own way of tying his umbilical cord to the next person's navel, whether that person is wealthy or penniless, a celebrity or an anonymous fan."

"Yes, Raul," Sid mumbled, hesitant to break his friend's magical spell. "Our buddy Manny Pacquiao must be the happiest man in the world!"

Raul gazed back at the streets of Manila, with the remaining commuters elbowing other commuters out of the way.

"No, my friend," Raul whispered to no one in particular. "Tonight, I am happier than him."

LONDONDERRY
TENDERLOIN

Asthma, incapacitating and lung-obstructive asthma, was the reason Seth was not allowed into the military college. The college had acknowledged that, based on his high-school grades, Seth was a bright student, but they deemed him unable to handle the rigors and physical stress of military life. He had graduated from a private military high school, rising to the rank of sergeant in the school's corps of cadets. Paperwork had been his main task. He was neat and organized, so, despite his asthma, the school had seen him as the one best suited to do the job. Because of this, they had given him the rank of sergeant. After that, he had gone to business school instead, where he had excelled.

Seth's Steakhouse was his father's business; it was named after him. When he was born, his father, then a custom-cut butcher and meat-store owner, decided to open a restaurant right in the heart of Brooklyn, New York. The restaurant offered special-cut meats and chops that were turned into delectable steaks. Beef, pork, lamb, veal, chicken, and even venison and mutton were served along with sausages, which were made in-house. It had been a thriving business during most of Seth's twenty-seven years. Now he had a business degree, and his father had made him manager of the business.

"I want to change the name to Sgt. Seth's Steakhouse," he had suggested to his father the day he graduated from business school. He wanted to pitch that a manly, macho appetite for steaks could be indulged and satisfied at their restaurant. His dad agreed. And sure enough, those three letters they added caught the attention of male meat lovers, and diners multiplied moderately.

After the increase in customers, Seth had made another suggestion. "Let's change the cushions on the seats," he said. He thought that if they made the cushions thinner and less comfortable, they could turn the tables over more often. Once again, Seth was right. They saw that they could turn the tables over one or two more times in an evening to accommodate the increased clientele. But Seth was not done. Next, he looked at the menu.

The menu was an old-style list of cut meats with a few words to explain, but not define, the selection. For example, one item read:

> *Tenderloin—a unique, choice cut of marinated prime beef grilled to your liking $32*

Seth rewrote the menu to say this:

> *LONDONDERRY TENDERLOIN—a choice cut of prime beef from grass-fed, grazed cows of Londonderry and other New Hampshire farms, grilled in hickory embers $37*

Londonderry tenderloin was a big hit. Diners loved the excellent-quality meat from cows not injected with artificial growth hormones. They loved that juicy, savory, clean-meat, hickory-fire description. They loved the flavor, the tenderness, and the perfect grilling. They did not even complain that Seth had raised the price.

On any given night, the restaurant waiting room was full. Reservations had to be booked ten days in advance. They also opened a take-out window. Sergeant Seth's Steakhouse was doing great business. Even Seth's asthma was doing well. Except for a couple of severe attacks, most of his asthma episodes caused only mild discomfort that was easily addressed by his ready medications. Seth was leading a great business and single life, making good money, and dating some of the most beautiful women in town.

One bright Monday morning at nine o'clock, there was a phone call at the restaurant. Everyone was tired from working the very busy weekend, and they were now setting up for another dining day that would start at ten thirty, as it did every morning. But it was a persistent telephone ring, the kind that just kept on and would not stop. Seth finally picked up the phone and, as always, put on his pleasant-sounding business tone, unaware that it was a call that would change his life and his business.

"Sgt. Seth's Steakhouse!"

"Good morning. My name is Alfred, and I would like to book your restaurant for a party we are planning."

"Good morning! My name is Seth, and I am the owner. When is your party for?"

"June 24th, dinner."

"June 24th. Isn't that a special day in the Catholic calendar?"

"Yes, it is the feast day of Saint John the Baptist, and it is also my grand-uncle's birthday. His name is also John—Monsignor John Mallory of the New York Archdiocese."

"Wow! We are quite honored that you chose our restaurant for such a special occasion. How old will the monsignor be?"

"He will be seventy-nine years old."

"Wow again! God bless him! That is a nice, mature age. I hope I can live that long!"

"Me too!" Alfred said, and they both laughed. Then Alfred added, "Believe me, he is still very sharp and active."

"Okay, I was checking our schedule as we spoke, and that date is free. So I will book the monsignor's party for that date, which is three months from now. How many people are coming?

"As of my last count, twenty-nine are coming, all adults. I am expecting more."

"We can set you up in our special function room that holds fifty people," Seth informed him.

"Good. We'd love that!"

"I just need a two hundred fifty dollar nonrefundable deposit to hold the function room."

"Okay, no problem. Here is my Visa number," said Alfred. Seth took Alfred's credit-card information and ran it on the computer.

"Okay, Alfred, your deposit is good!"

"Good. Thanks!"

Seth paused for a moment and then asked a crucial question. "By the way, Alfred, I always ask this question of our customers. What made you choose our restaurant for this very special occasion?"

"About seven months ago, a group of us, including the monsignor, dined there, and he really loved your Londonderry Tenderloin. He told us he has been there a few times since then. So, we're taking him back for the Londonderry Tenderloin. We all loved the food and the sound of that name, Londonderry Tenderloin."

"Thank you very much. I was the one who named it that."

They were about to close the conversation when Alfred had a question. "By the way, Seth, did you serve in the military? The name of your restaurant is Sergeant Seth's Steakhouse."

"I went to a military high school in New Hampshire where I was the sergeant of the cadet corps. I never went on active duty."

"I asked because I was in the Marine Corps for eight years. Currently I practice law in Manhattan."

"That's good to know."

"So if you need any kind of legal help, please let me know."

"Okay. When that time comes, I will definitely call you, Alfred; thank you very much for the business!" They hung up.

The two men spoke a few more times to finalize the party details. During those conversations, they found each other witty and engaging and became good phone friends—so good that Seth gave Alfred a 15 percent discount on their future party bill.

Alfred, in turn, gave Seth free legal advice on some restaurant concerns.

But early friendship, untested and untried, could be disarming. Their comfortable banter moved on to subjects that were not meant to be mentioned, no matter how casually.

"You know, Seth, your employees are very pleasant and friendly. You must pay them quite well!" Alfred remarked.

"I hire undocumented workers—the best workers for the money. They make good tips every night." Seth laughed innocently as he bragged about his hiring policy, not knowing that his cold, cruel tone stunned the law practitioner in Alfred. To Seth, it was just another of his astute business secrets.

Although the two men hadn't yet met, each one tried to draw a composite profile of the other based on his phone voice alone. Seth saw Alfred as a muscular former marine, about six feet tall, articulate, and well dressed. His manners had been refined by the practice of law; he was confident and secure. Alfred saw Seth as average in weight and height, stylish and well dressed, shrewd, and also confident and secure. They could not wait to meet.

Sgt. Seth's Steakhouse sat in a crowded, commercial part of Brooklyn with just about one other competing steak house every three blocks. When Seth took over the business, he had chosen a light-beige interior wallpaper, on which he had hung black frames with colorful Picasso style paintings, giving the place a very classy look. He had then put up a wall-sized mirror to cover the busy, noisy grill area. The mirror illuminated the bar and dining room. Around the neighborhood, the whiff of grilled meats spread from the chimney smoke, inviting everyone to dine in.

June 24th finally arrived. It was the night for Monsignor John Mallory's big birthday party. He wore his priestly black suit with a black shirt and white collar. He was tall, more than six feet, and had a medium build with a reddish round face and thinning hair on top. He had a loud, contagious laugh that boomed through the room all night. He was so happy to meet Seth.

"How are you, Sergeant Seth?" His big, strong hands gripped Seth's hand as they shook.

"Thank you, monsignor, for choosing our restaurant for your birthday party!"

"Oh, I have been here a few times, and I've always had a craving for your Londonderry Tenderloin ever since I first tasted it."

"That's great, monsignor. I'll make sure you get a nice juicy one tonight!"

Alfred walked in the front door and saw Seth just as Seth was about to greet him. They recognized each other immediately. They both knew instantly that their profiles of each other were correct. It was a long handshake for the two party planners.

Cocktails were flowing, hors d'oeuvres were float-ing, and laughter filled the function room as the well-dressed guests mingled. There were a few men wearing the priestly white collar, and one of them Seth recognized as the archbishop. The archbishop asked the people to quiet down as he spoke some opening greetings for the honored guest.

"I want to thank the Mallory family for inviting me to the monsignor's birthday party. Monsignor Mallory continues to serve the faithful of New York every day with unwavering passion and dedica-tion. And each day that we can tap into his wisdom and enthusiasm is a day we can all thank God for." The room was silent as the archbishop paused, un-able to speak because he was so emotional. The crowd felt the warmth of his unplanned tears. Then he smiled deviously, bounced back, and spoke again: "I remember one piece of advice that he gave me was when he said, 'Father, you have to try the Londonderry tenderloin at Sergeant Seth's Steakhouse!'" The room erupted with wild, loud laughter and applause. The archbishop was still laughing as he said, "Hey, I don't want to bore you with a long speech; after we have our steaks, we can go ahead to roast and toast our beloved monsignor all we want." Laughter and applause were again heard in the room.

The servers brought out the appetizers first, fol-lowed by the soup. A Caucasian waitress was busy serving Alfred's table, all the while smiling at the seated guests. Alfred could not help but ask.

"You're a very good server, miss. What is your name?"

"My name is Olga." She smiled sweetly and shyly, which brought out her beautiful face as she spoke. Alfred guessed that she must be about thirty years old.

"Your accent sounds Russian. Am I right?"

"Yes, I am from Ukraine." She kept smiling.

"The reason I know is that I have clients that are from Russia, I'm a lawyer." The waitress nodded and smiled back at Alfred to acknowledge what he had said.

The laughter and voices were muffled by the clink of shining silverware in the guests' mouths. The appetizer and soup were delicious; the guests were all nodding their heads in agreement. Alfred continued to talk to the waitress.

"You know, Olga, I noticed that the workers here are very friendly and courteous."

"Thank you, sir, we try!"

"Seth must be a good boss, huh?"

"We all love Mr. Seth for giving us a chance to work here." She kept smiling. Alfred kept probing.

"Were you also a waitress in Ukraine?" Alfred felt the elbow of his wife in his side.

"You're asking too many questions," a bit annoyed, she reminded Alfred.

Olga replied, "I worked as a pharmacist there."

"Wow, that's a good-paying job!" Alfred's wife remarked.

"I still have to pass the test to be licensed here; right now I am reviewing for it," Olga said as she kept her smile.

Alfred appreciated the fervor and honesty of this Ukrainian immigrant working hard to improve her life.

"Is your family here, Olga?" Alfred's wife asked.

"No, they're still in Ukraine. I need to concentrate on my studies so I live alone for now, but I promised I would bring them here when I get my license."

Alfred had a newfound respect for Seth as a businessman for knowing how to pick his restaurant help. Seth selected the motivated, reliable, and educated immigrants as employees. They never disappointed.

It was now time to bring in the main course. The meats sizzled as they were served, filling the room with the aroma of marinated grilled beef. Almost everyone had ordered the Londonderry Tenderloin. As soon as the plates landed in front of them, the guests started to cut and chew, and again they nodded in praise. Monsignor Mallory and the archbishop, two big Irishmen who sat next to each other, briefly kept quiet as they allowed their gusto for meat and potatoes to take charge. Everyone was pleased and content.

Then, the colorful desserts were served. There were a few to choose from, all designed to leave a sweet aftertaste following the savory meal. Next, the microphones started to get busy again. One by one, the guests took the opportunity to roast and toast the celebrant, mentioning his virtues and their memories of him. The speeches were sentimental, funny, and sweet. Some roasters found themselves with tears in their eyes, unable to speak. Alfred was one of the last ones up. He walked to the microphone knowing that his tribute to his old dear grand uncle tonight could be his last, due to his old age.

"As I was getting dressed to come here, I thought I'd wear my Marine Corps uniform and give my uncle John a sharp marine salute. Uncle John was a marine too, before going to the seminary. So I tried on my uniform. It was a struggle. Once I got it on, I looked in the mirror, and I looked ridiculous." Everybody laughed.

"When my brother Allan and I we were in our early teens, I remember Uncle John caught us reading a *Playboy* magazine. We were very curious kids. Uncle John sat us down and advised us that it's okay to be curious but not to allow ourselves to indulge in the dark temptations that are in those fleshy pages." Everyone was quiet. Alfred continued.

"At my high-school graduation, I was not sure which direction I would go next. Uncle John advised me to join the US Marines. I was a basketball player, and I had good grades; he said I could use those God-given gifts in the Marine Corps as I contemplated my future. I took his advice. My eight years in the Marine Corps were some of the best years of my early manhood." There was some applause.

"My uncle John became my father-confessor. Whenever I needed advice on big decisions in my life, I would go see him. He would give me advice that I knew came from his ever-brilliant mind and from the innermost corner of his loving, compassionate heart. And I know he does that for every one of us in this archdiocese who seeks his counsel." Everyone was in tears. Alfred had to pause to wipe the tears from his eyes. He concluded by saying, "To my beloved uncle John. This salute is for you!" Alfred kicked his heels, stood at military attention, and gave the monsignor a prolonged Marine Corps salute.

No one was more moved by Alfred's speech than Seth was. Growing up, he did not have an uncle or great-uncle to guide him the same way Alfred had been guided. And that Marine Corps salute! As a sergeant in the high-school cadet corps, he had been given the salute by lower-ranked cadets. He missed that kind of symbolic respect; the absence of military order remained a frustration for him.

Everybody stood up to applaud Alfred for his tribute to his grand-uncle. Then the monsignor stood up, assisted by Alfred as he slowly walked to the microphone.

"As you all know, I am seventy-nine years old today. When you are an old priest, you are in consultation with your creator about when the best time for you to go. And we've had some back and forth on the subject." He had a devious smile. "I said to my creator, 'You can take me anytime, but not before I've had my last bite of my Londonderry Tenderloin.'" Everybody laughed, and the monsignor went on to deliver the rest of his speech.

As the monsignor spoke, Seth walked towards Alfred's table to shake his hand. "Great tribute, Alfred!"

"Thanks," Alfred replied. "He's a great hero to me!"

In the midst of their handshake, Seth felt his chest tighten and his breath shorten. An asthma attack was forthcoming. Right away, Seth pulled out his inhaler from his pocket and placed it into his mouth. He started pumping. This was not a good sign at all. His asthma attacks usually preceded a terrible, terrible occurrence. At that moment, he clearly recalled the asthma attack he'd had before the small fire that had gutted the grill side of the kitchen. Then there was the asthma attack that had happened before the big fistfight between two groups of customers over a parking space. Alfred helped Seth settle on a chair so he could keep using his pump followed by heavy puffs of medicinal air.

Seth was starting to feel the relief of fresh oxygen in his lungs when they heard a loud noise. It sounded like a live microphone had been dropped on the floor. The ladies started screaming. The male guests rushed to the monsignor, who they had seen collapse as he was giving his thank-you speech. Seth and Alfred ran toward the old priest too. One doctor tried chest compressions and mouth-to-mouth resuscitation, but the monsignor lay on the floor motionless. He was dead.

The next day's headlines read, "MONSIGNOR JOHN MALLORY, 1937–2016." Seth's Steakhouse was mentioned in the news as the place where he had collapsed and died. It was embarrassing to be at the forefront of the day's negative news, Seth thought. The restaurant was quiet and slow for the next few days as it started to lose customers.

The Mallory family was very understanding in their grief. Most of them felt that there was no need to do an autopsy on the monsignor since the authorities had concluded that he died of natural causes due to his old age. It was Alfred who insisted on doing an autopsy. He had some nagging negative feelings about the cause of death.

He was right to suspect something. The autopsy found that Monsignor Mallory had suffered sudden cardiac arrest, in which his heart had suddenly stopped beating. It had not been a heart attack. There were several factors that may have caused it. Among the possibilities was an interaction between his medications and the amount of alcohol he had consumed that evening and the intensity of the high and low emotions he had experienced. But the investigation also revealed some information that proved damning for Seth.

It revealed small traces of synthetic growth hormones and bovine antibiotics in the monsignor. Alfred found out that the synthetic growth hormones can cause mastitis, a breast infection, in cows and that this infection requires treatment with antibiotics. What the autopsy revealed, then, was that Seth was serving inferior-quality beef instead of beef from prime, grass-fed, grazed cows from the organic farms of New Hampshire, as he had proudly advertised.

The Mallory family decided to sue Seth and his restaurant for fraud for mislabeling their products. That lawsuit was followed by suits from the New York attorney general, the New Hampshire Beef Industry Council, and the state of New Hampshire. The negative publicity proved fatal for Seth's business. Customers stayed away from the restaurant. It quickly filed for bankruptcy and never recovered.

About a month after his restaurant closed, Seth went back to the neighborhood where it had been. He stood across the street from the closed doors. He saw the bright yellow police tape on the door to attest that it was a crime scene. There was no aromatic smoke coming out of its chimney anymore. There was only the shell of a business that once thrived on goodwill and patronage. He was in the midst of thinking about a comeback when he heard a sweet, familiar voice.

"Hi, boss!"

Seth turned and saw Olga by his side. "Oh, hi, Olga!" Hers was a welcome voice for Seth's gloomy mood.

"I just passed the state pharmacy test, Seth, thanks to you!" She was very excited.

"Very good, Olga! Congratulations!" They hugged as they shared the good news. Seth added, "We would have had a party for you if we still had the restaurant." He looked at the restaurant's closed doors.

"I know, Seth. But don't worry. Today, I'm buying you brunch." She tugged at Seth's right arm and started walking, but Seth stayed where he was, not wanting to move.

"What are you thinking, Seth?" she asked.

"I was thinking, Olga, that if it had been a dreaded gangster who had died at our restaurant instead of the monsignor, our restaurant would have been notoriously famous!" They both laughed, and Olga nodded her head in polite agreement.

"Always an astute angle, huh, Seth?" she complimented her ex-boss.

Seth smiled at her and winked. "Always!"

BLUEPRINT FOR A BORDELLO

There was a handwritten Post-it note on Ron's desk when he arrived at work on a warm Monday morning in August. It was from his boss, Mack Higgins, one of the partners in the architectural firm where Ron worked. Mack was his mentor, the man who had hired him and who guided and critiqued him through his insecurities. Mack also backed Ron when he had to navigate the challenging politics of the firm. He owed Mack. Mack could be a tough boss, but he was known to be fair and respected in the business that bore his name. Ron knew he had to see Mack right away.

"Come in, Ron, and close the door!" Mack was on the phone. He pointed to a chair facing his desk, which Ron settled into, and then continued what seemed like a funny, friendly phone conversation with a deep male voice on the other end. Ron could hear the other man laughing. Mack chuckled when the man spoke, causing Ron to smile at the cheerfulness of the ongoing exchange. He and Mack were the only ones in the room. He looked back at the door to see whether anyone else was joining them. Curiosity and some anxiety filled his thoughts. In their collaborative design business, there was usually a team of architects to be briefed on a new project. He waited quietly as Mack ended his phone call, promising the man they would talk again.

"That was my best friend, Larry, from Nevada. He just gave us a new project." Ron could see the excitement in Mack's face. Mack wore a light-purple, striped tie over a light-blue shirt that showed the slight tan he had gotten over the weekend. He looked relaxed and had a grin on his face. A new project always made him excited.

"Before we start business, how was your sermon yesterday, Deacon Ron?" Everyone in the firm knew that Ron was an ordained deacon at his Catholic church. The diaconate task seemed just right for the soft-spoken, mild-mannered family man. But parishioners had noted that his sermons were, at best, bland. Bland—much like hospital meat loaf. Oftentimes, he cited uninteresting analogies that steered listeners into restlessness and boredom. And Ron knew it.

"They seemed to like it. I really hope they did," Ron humbly replied. Mack then went right into business.

"I know you're working on three projects right now, Ron, but I want you to concentrate on Larry's design. I might have to turn over your other jobs to Bill, because this is very important for me. Larry is my best friend," Mack said, and Ron nodded in agreement.

"Sure, Mack, no problem," Ron replied with enthusiasm.

"Just to introduce to you who Larry is, we met in high-school priesthood seminary class. Our parents wanted us to be priests, and at that time we thought we wanted to be priests too. But we both realized early enough that neither of us had that priestly calling. Seminary work was too rigid for both of us. So, after two years, we left. We've been best friends ever since."

"You turned out okay, Mack. How about Larry?"

"Oh, I think he turned out way better than I did. He has no worry lines on his face, and he became very wealthy," Mack said as he laughed, leaving Ron with a questioning face.

"What does he do now?"

"He owns a bordello in Nevada," Mack replied, waiting for Ron's reaction.

"Bordello?" Ron knew the word but was doubtful that he'd heard it correctly.

"A prostitution house, if I may simplify it for you, Deacon Ron," Mack said as he kept smiling, amused at the reeducation of his friend the deacon.

"Oh, I know that!" Ron attempted to look better informed. He continued, saying, "So, from the seminary, Larry went into the bordello business?"

"Well, he did a few other things, mainly in Las Vegas. And now he is our client."

"Okay! I think we can design whatever bordello he wants." Ron wanted the challenge.

"I picked you for this job because I saw your work on the Picard Family Resort in Memphis. That was a great design, and our clients were very pleased," Mack said, beaming with pride.

"Thanks, Mack, but you already told me that."

"Now I want my buddy Larry to be pleased too. I told him I'd pick my best architect to do the job." Mack tapped Ron's hands to complete the compliment.

"I'll do my best, Mack."

"Great!" Mack said. He pulled out a brown Manila envelope from his desk and handed it to Ron.

"Here are the cadastral maps Larry sent me. See if you can give me some initial drawings in two days.

I want to see them, and Larry wants to see them too. He also wants you to work with the surveyor to make sure you can come up with a good design."

"Why? Is it a new property?"

"Yes. He bought a new property that is three times the size of his old one. He wants a resort-like feel for this new bordello, with steam baths and massage rooms for a completely relaxing environment for his customers." Mack made air quotes with his fingers as he described Larry's specs. He winked at Ron.

"Really!" Ron remembered his previous resort work, which made him excited too.

"Yes! Pack your bags, because you're headed to Nevada in two days," Mack said, and he tapped Ron's back, confident he had picked a good architect for the job.

Ron went home that night excited to have another new solo project. His wife, Ellen, noticed the excitement on his face, and he told her he had a new project in Nevada but did not go into details. At dinner, he told his three young daughters that he would be going to Nevada on business. His daughters were aware of the travel part of his job.

"Isn't Nevada where Las Vegas is, Dad?" asked Millie, the ten-year-old middle child.

"Yes, but I'm not going to Las Vegas. I'm going about thirty miles north of Las Vegas," Ron explained.

"Don't you want to see Las Vegas, Dad?" asked Eleanor, the eldest daughter and an altar server in their church.

"No, sweetheart. You all know how I feel about gambling. I only play quarter poker with your uncles."

"Can you bring me a candle from a church in Nevada, Dad?" Rona, the youngest daughter, asked.

"Sure, honey, that's an easy request. I'll see if I can find a church near the site of the bor..." He had almost slipped! He scooped a big helping of mashed potatoes with his spoon, quickly brought a bite to his mouth, and started chewing.

"What's the site of the bor...?" Ellen asked. The unfinished sentence had caught her attention.

"That's the borough where I'm headed. I'll see if there is a church near that borough where I can get the candles," he said, and he felt relieved at his quick thinking.

"Get me a candle too, Daddy," Millie demanded.

"Me too, Dad," Eleanor said.

"No problem, but let me ask you: why the sudden liking for candles?" Ron said to his daughters.

"I don't want you to miss Sunday Mass, Dad. You might get too busy," said Rona.

"I'll make sure I go to Sunday Mass and get your candles, and I'll talk to you on Skype in the evenings, like we always do when I'm out of town."

As he and Ellen got their daughters ready for bed, Ron recalled the early years of their marriage. He and Ellen had been college sweethearts. He'd started as a draftsman for Mack during his senior year at architectural college. Mack had taken a liking to the dedicated student, who saw the contour of a piece of land as a canvas for his designs. Ron preferred designing hotels and recreational resorts more than urban high-rises because he loved the earth. He always insisted on recommending the landscaping of trees and foliage as essential to his designs.

It was their church pastor who had convinced Ron, a very active member of their church, to study to become a deacon. He and Ellen had both gone to Catholic high schools. They had become good church leaders as well.

As they lay in bed after the long day, Ron told Ellen about his new project. Unsurprisingly, she was concerned.

"A bordello? With prostitutes? Are you serious, Ronald?"

"I'm an architect, Ellen. I go where the jobs are." He had to calm her down.

"I am curious why Mack gave you this job, knowing you're a church deacon."

"The client is his best friend. He told me I was the best designer for the job, and I was flattered to get it." His explanation was reassuring enough for Ellen.

"The girls and I will pray that you don't get into any bit of temptation."

"We've been married thirteen years, dear. You know me better than that."

"Those wild girls could be very tempting, Ron. The flesh is weak!"

The next day, Ron showed Mack his initial sketches based on the cadastral maps. Mack liked them, and again he told Ron that he was the right man for the job. The sketches were sent to Larry, who also liked them. But there were some specs that Larry wanted to discuss personally with the architect. So Ron was on a plane to Nevada that Friday afternoon.

On the plane, Ron bowed his head and prayed. "Dear God, I pray for courage and strength. Please do not allow me to the temptation test. I know that, where I am headed, I will see scantily clad women or maybe women who aren't clad at all. My faith is firm and uncompromising. I'm sure you know that. But, should I falter and fall into sin, give me a clear and compelling lesson for my weakness and an honest resolve to reconcile with you. Amen."

Then he remembered his daughters' requests for candles. Why candles? He wondered. They'd always asked for chocolates and T-shirts when he'd gone on trips, but this time it was candles. The requests had started with seven-year-old Rona, who they noticed had always had a keen sense of perception and intuition. Rona could guess the outcome of a ball game without even knowing the team and the players. "The brown shirts will win!" she would guess, and she was right 95 percent of the time. Ron missed her little voice already. He dismissed the candles from his mind as he looked out the plane window. He reclined his seat, closed his eyes, and drifted into a light sleep for the rest of the flight.

Ron arrived at Nevada's McCarran International Airport at about nine in the evening. He saw the slot machines by the waiting lounges, busy with their blinking lights, musical bells, and fake coin sounds. Winning at the slot machines at the airport after you arrive could be a great lucky start. Losing, of course, could be a bad omen. Ron was tempted to pull out a twenty-dollar bill and try his luck. Instead, he kept walking toward the luggage carousel. Temptation, he thought, could be managed. A tall, smiling gentleman holding Ron's name on a piece of cardboard greeted him, took his bags, and then led him to a long, black car.

"Have you been to Las Vegas, Mr. Ron?" the driver asked him.

"No, not yet."

"Mr. Larry instructed me to drive you through the Strip, just to show you where the big casinos are."

"Okay, I don't mind. Thanks."

Ron saw the bright lights, the water fountains, the Eiffel Tower replica, and all the symbols that set each casino apart. He felt no urge to go in any of them. He also saw the drive-thru chapels and the signs with scantily clad men and women for hire alongside big, bright phone numbers. It was a place where one's carnal desires could be sought and bought, for the right price. He recalled the words of his youngest daughter's request for church candles; he would have to get those candles to prove to them he was in church where they expected him to be.

About forty minutes past the Strip, the driver pointed to a one-story building on the left with a bright neon sign that read "Temptress Ranch."

"That's Mr. Larry's bordello," the driver said.

"It looks very busy. I see a lot of cars," Ron observed.

"Yes, most customers usually come in at this time."

After twenty more minutes, the car made a right turn onto a road in a dark, wide-open desert land. There were no streetlights. Then he saw a big, illuminated house on the right about a quarter mile from the road. It was the only lit property around.

"Is this Larry's mansion?" Ron asked.

"Yes, sir!"

As he opened the car door, Ron heard dogs barking. He then saw a tall, heavyset man come out of the main door. The man was wearing a green plaid long-sleeved shirt and smoking a cigar. He smiled at Ron and seemed glad to see him.

"Hi, Ron. I'm Larry. Welcome to Nevada." They shook hands, and Larry led him inside his house.

"Is this where you plan to build it?" Ron asked.

"Yes, we have forty-three acres of desert land on the side and in the back that's waiting to be developed. And I know you'll help me do that." Larry puffed his cigar and exhaled upward to avoid Ron's face. "But I know you're tired from the flight, so we'll talk tomorrow. I have to go the ranch. It's a very busy night over there." He tapped Ron on the shoulder. Ron remembered the same hand tap he'd gotten from Mack.

"My maid will show you to your room. If you need anything such as food or pajamas, just let the maid know and she'll get it for you." They shook hands again, and then Larry went out to the big car that was waiting for him and drove off.

The maid led him upstairs to his bedroom. As he walked through the hallway, he saw framed pictures on the wall of nine pretty women. They wore revealing clothes and posed provocatively, their lips flaunting kisses to the camera lens. Very sexy, Ron thought.

"These are all of Larry's girlfriends, past and present," the maid said.

"Wow!" Ron said, but he was not shocked anymore. He realized that Larry's world was very far removed from his world of family, work, and prayer. The mansion was filled with designer furniture and expensive-looking works of "nudes" art. There were portraits of nudes in oil, watercolor, and charcoal. He found no books or mature periodicals like *Time* that may have suggested some interest in the humanities. Not one.

Ron asked the maid for a grilled-cheese sandwich and a glass of milk, as he was a bit hungry. The maid brought them promptly. Exhausted, he fell asleep right away after eating.

Ron's cell-phone alarm sounded at 2:00 a.m. It woke him up from a deep sleep. He had forgotten to reset it to account for the three-hour time lag between the East Coast and the West Coast. He silenced it and tried to go back to sleep, but he couldn't. He got up and looked out the window. Except for some small ground lights, the exterior was all dark—no sign of neighboring houses or passing cars. Ron walked toward the illuminated hallway again where Larry's girlfriends' pictures were hung. It was the last picture, presumably of Larry's current girlfriend, that had caught his attention. She was a pretty brunette, so strikingly pretty and barely dressed in a scanty, two-piece swimsuit. He looked closely at her dark-brown eyes. As provocatively as she had tried to pose for that picture, her eyes showed a hint of sadness, Ron thought. He looked at the picture for another five minutes and then went back to sleep.

While Ron was having breakfast, the maid told him that Larry was still sleeping. Larry left instructions explaining that the surveyor would be coming shortly so that both Ron and the surveyor could work on the field and do the second survey. The weather was too hot and dry for Ron, so the maid packed ice-cold water bottles in a cooler for Ron to take with him. But the heat was just too much for both men. They doused the cold bottled water on themselves for relief.

Ron went back to Larry's mansion after the grueling three-hour survey. His cotton shirt and pants were soaked with sweat; he was tired and dripping. He found Larry having coffee with a pretty brunette, the same brunette girl he had seen in the girlfriends' pictures. Larry was wearing just his white boxer shorts with his big belly hanging out and his hairy chest exposed. The brunette wore a short pink satin robe revealing a startling amount of cleavage, but she didn't seem to mind that Ron quickly glanced at it.

"Hi, Ron. This is my girlfriend, Bridget," Larry said, and then he introduced Ron. "Bridget, this is Ron, my architect." They said quick hellos to each other, and then Ron went upstairs to shower and change. On his way back to his room, he passed by the last picture again and said to himself, "God, she is beautiful."

Lunch was being served when Ron came down. Larry was now wearing a yellow cotton golf shirt. Bridget wore a tight pair of jeans and a matching blue strapless blouse. During lunch, Larry and Bridget gave Ron the specs of their vision for the brand-new bordello.

Their instructions to Ron were as follows:

- There will have to be some distance between Larry's mansion and the bordello, with big green cactus plants separating the two estates.
- A short, covered, illuminated stone bridge will allow access to both properties.
- There will be a bigger office space for Larry and his staff.
- There will be a circular liquor bar for the customers.
- There will be a wider "line-up" lounge area for the girls.
- There will be ten additional party rooms, which will be bigger than the old ones.

Business looks very good, Ron thought.

"Don't forget my room 13," Bridget reminded Larry.

"Ah, yes," Larry said. "Room 13 will be the biggest party room, with special panels, plush carpet, a Jacuzzi, and fine furnishings. Customers will pay a premium to be in room 13, which will be Bridget's party room." Ron managed a smile as he took notes. He could see the excitement on Bridget's pretty face.

Larry looked at his watch and remembered something. "I have a meeting with my banker," he said as he headed upstairs. Looking at his girlfriend, he asked, "Bridget, honey, why don't you take Ron to the ranch and show him around? I will be back around four o'clock."

After lunch, Bridget led Ron to her BMW sports car. As she drove, she directed charming questions to the timid, overwhelmed architect.

"I heard you're a church deacon, Ron?"

"Yes," he replied, and he wished he could say more. He looked at her smooth, bare shoulders but was afraid to stare. "I like it," he added.

"This bordello business might be a bit too revealing for a deacon like you, Ron, especially the skin show," she said, smiling. "Wearing less and showing our bare bodies is how we make a living," she continued. "And we like it too," she added.

"Well, that's okay; we all have to make a living." Ron laughed in polite agreement. Then Bridget shared some information on herself.

"I used to work for an interior decorator, so I will be managing the construction of the new bordello, Ron. We will be working closely with each other, so I want us to work well together." She took her eyes off the road to look at Ron. "If there's anything you feel you have to tell me, or if you have any questions or any situations, just let me know. Okay, Ron?" She took her right hand off the wheel and caressed Ron's shoulder, and then she offered to shake his hand. They shook hands. Ron felt relieved of his initial anxiety; he felt more relaxed with her after that handshake. Excitement took over him at the thought of working with this very pretty girl.

"I'd like to stop at the florist to get fresh flowers for the ranch," Bridget said.

"That's okay with me. I have time!" Ron was having fun. All he could think of was Bridget.

Bridget picked several bunches of red roses that she planned to give to each of the girls at the Temptress Ranch. Next, they stopped at the cleaners to pick up some dry-cleaned, expensive-looking women's clothes. Afterward they went to the pharmacy to pick up medication for Larry. Ron was gallantly in tow.

"Is there anything you need, Ron, while we're here?"

"No, nothing, thanks," he replied. But there was something that Ron truly wanted. He did not want this lovely moment with pretty Bridget to end.

As they loaded the items into the car, Bridget was gracious. "Ron, thank you for being patient. Larry has no patience for these little errands." She walked toward him to touch his chest and gave him a quick kiss on the lips. He froze for a moment. The kiss was unexpected. His heart started to beat faster. A very lovely moment indeed.

They arrived at the Temptress Ranch, where the scantily clad girls were delighted to see the flowers. Bridget introduced Ron to them.

"Girls, this is Architect Ron. He will give you each a flower, so make sure you thank him with a nice, wet

Temptress kiss!" Bridget instructed. And one by one they did, all eighteen of them. Ron's face was covered with lipstick.

It was about five in the afternoon, and some male customers were starting to come in. Bridget wanted to change into her "work clothes" and needed Ron's help.

"Ron, could you please get my pink outfit from the car and bring it to room 13?"

"Okay," Ron replied and quickly went to the car. He looked at the dry-cleaned outfit and thought, it's not much of an outfit. A tiny, pink bikini top and matching short skirt that would barely cover her. He knocked on room 13 and heard Bridget's voice say, "Come in."

Bridget was seated at her dressing table fixing her hair. Her back was facing Ron, but from the mirror in front of her, Ron could see her bare upper body very clearly. Ron timidly tried not to stare. It was at this time that his cell phone rang. When he answered, his wife sounded very frustrated.

"Ron, I called you a few times. Did you get my messages?"

"No, honey. I'm sorry. I have been very busy," he said as he took a deep breath.

"The girls wanted to talk to you, but they're in bed now. It's nine thirty here."

"It's only six thirty here. I was working under the sun for most of the day today and I didn't hear my phone ring. Are you all okay?" Ron did not want to mention any reference to family that Bridget might hear.

"Your college classmate Alberto called. I gave him your phone number."

"Okay, thanks. I'll wait for his call."

"When are you coming back?"

"I don't know yet; my work is not yet done. I'll let you know, okay?" Ron wanted to end the conversation right away. He felt some guilt that he would rather be in Bridget's company at the moment, but Bridget was all he had on his mind.

While he had been on the phone, he'd seen Bridget get up from her dresser to take out the pink outfit. He'd seen she was wearing a G-string and nothing else. Now Bridget took the outfit out of the cleaners' plastic cover and put it on, knowing quite well that Ron was watching.

"Ron, can you please look at my back and see how this fits?"

"It looks very good on you. You look very pretty!" Ron could not help but give her the compliment. Immodestly, she exposed her curves, her silky skin, and her high-priced femininity—all were there for him to view up close. She did not seem to mind him looking at her. She was even encouraging.

"I'd like to take a picture of us!" said Bridget. Ron could not say no. Bridget took out her cell phone, placed her arm around Ron, and snapped two shots.

It was the first time they had been that close to each other. He knew he was at liberty to touch her and kiss her, and, at that moment, he was very much tempted to. But then he heard his cell phone sound. Bridget had sent the picture to his cell phone. "Now we both have a souvenir of your trip here," Bridget said.

Ron could not sleep that night. He kept looking at the picture with Bridget on his cell phone. Hers was a seductive smile and pose; she was quite a temptation. He recalled that moment when their upper bodies had touched tightly as he wrapped her arms around his waist to make sure their bodies were connected for the selfie. Nothing else was on his mind but her.

It was about one o'clock in the morning when Ron's cell phone rang. His phone was still lit with the picture of Bridget when the incoming image showed his home phone. It was his youngest daughter.

"Daddy, I can't sleep!" Rona's tiny voice bore through his ear like a drill. He refocused on his daughter.

"What's the matter, Rona? Are you hungry?" he asked, sounding concerned.

"I had a bad dream," the tiny, piercing voice said.

"Do you want to tell me about it?"

"I dreamed about this big, big blackbird that flew over you when you were working in the field and took you away from us!" She started to cry.

"You don't have to worry about me, honey. I'm very much okay. I'm in my room alone trying to plan my day tomorrow." He remembered the candles. "Tomorrow is Sunday, honey. I'll try to find a church nearby and get you the candles you wanted. See, I haven't forgotten."

"I was going to tell you about those candles. I thought you forgot." She stopped crying.

"I didn't forget, honey. Those candles are always on my mind." It was a lie.

"I just wanted to hear your voice, Dad." Rona sounded better.

"Okay, dear, go to sleep now. And I want you to wear your favorite yellow dress for Mass tomorrow. Good night!" He tried to sound upbeat and reassuring.

"Good night, Dad!"

Ron felt even guiltier for lying to his daughter. Bridget, not the candles, was always on his mind. But the thought of Bridget and a lit candle caught his imagination. Could Bridget somehow be similar to a lit candle? The idea stopped and emptied Ron's mind. His thoughts shifted to this idea of Bridget and the lit candle. He asked himself, Are they similar? How are they similar, or are they in total conflict with each other?

Ron remembered that Bridget's seductive pose was hot, like she was on fire. And the lit candle with a small, flickering flame came back to mind. He thought how similar the two could be. Could there be some hope for Bridget to get out of this flesh trade? She was smart, and she was young. She could find another, more decent line of work, or could she? And would she want to? In the midst of these questions, his cell phone rang again. It was his college buddy.

"Hello. Is this Ron?"

"Alberto!"

"Yes, Ron, how did you know?"

"Your name lit up on my phone, and, besides, I will never forget your raspy voice."

"We never even saw each other again after our class reunion six years ago!"

"Yes. I'm here in Nevada on a project, Al."

"So am I. I'm here at the Strip! Can you believe it? We're both here! For some reason, there was something pushing me to call you. I called your house, and Ellen said you were here, so she gave me your cell phone. Sorry to call you so late."

"I'll always take your call, Al. Any time, buddy."

Ron suddenly thought of something. "Listen, Al, thank you for calling me. I need to go to a church tomorrow for Sunday Mass. Are you close to a church where you are now?"

"Yes, there's a church about two blocks away from my hotel."

"Great! Did you rent a car? Do you think you can take me there?"

"Yes. Where are you staying?"

"I'm staying at my client's mansion, about thirty miles from the Strip. Can you pick me up?"

"No problem, buddy. Do you want to catch the ten o'clock Mass?"

"Yes, the ten o'clock Mass is good. We can then have brunch after and catch up. I'll text you the address. You saved my life, Al. You have no idea. Thanks so much, and I'll see you in the morning."

The Mass that Sunday was intensely special for Ron. It was like salvation. He knew he was smitten with Bridget and had fallen so quickly for her charms. For a while, he had forgotten about his family as he flirted with the delightfully alluring idea that the two of them could find romance—some hot, passionate, momentary romance. He had thought briefly of staying in room 13 as Bridget's lover for the evening. But the three church candles had proven that the idea was plain silly. He could not imagine turning away from his family and the deacon role he had worked so hard for.

Ron was back at the mansion at three in the afternoon with an entirely different mind-set. Bridget was in the pool keeping cool from the very hot sun.

"I need to talk to you, Bridget." Ron's face was serious. He felt and showed no excitement at the sight of her bare body. Bridget noticed this, and she covered her wet two-piece swimsuit with a bathrobe. They sat under a shaded, open umbrella.

"Yes, Ron?" She didn't try to flirt.

"I'm worried about you, Bridget, in this job that you do." Bridget could see the concern in Ron's face.

"Don't worry about me, Ron. I'll be okay!" She took a sip of a cold fruit drink, brushing off his concern for her.

"Bridget, you're only good in this job when you're young. What happens in five years when you've aged?"

"I'll worry about that in five years, Ron." She looked away from him.

"Bridget, I saw the sadness in your eyes the first time I saw your picture. The uncertainty and sadness of your life were visible. You cannot deny that," Ron persisted.

"I'm not as smart as you are, Architect Ron. I struggled to finish high school." She put on her dark glasses to hide her eyes from Ron's. "There are no jobs that pay as well and as easy as this." Bridget dismissed him, but Ron persisted.

"Do you ever think of your family, Bridget?"

"Why should I care? They don't even keep in touch. Larry is the only family I have."

Ron took a deep breath to help him explain. "Bridget, you are like a candle burning quickly on both ends," he told her. "I know Larry gives you some comforting security at the moment, but we both know he could also drop you any time a prettier girl comes along."

Bridget was quiet. She knew Ron was right. Her future with Larry was as secure as the thin G-string she wore to please him. Ron was now getting through to her.

"Listen, Bridget, I have a friend who is an architect in San Diego. His wife is an interior decorator—and a very successful one too. I spoke to them about you, and his wife said she was willing to meet you and see how she could help." Ron paused to look straight into her eyes. "Just give it a try—a good serious effort, Bridget. My friend Al and his wife are honest people. They are willing to help you and not exploit you like the johns you meet on the job!" Ron paused to catch his breath; he was persistent. "Bridget, if you look into this, I will pray for your success every day, the same way I pray for my family. And I will be there to support you any way I can!" Ron finally stopped when he saw Bridget tear up. She wiped the tears beneath her dark eyeglasses with her terry-cloth robe. Only her sobs could be heard in the silence that followed. She finally nodded her head in agreement.

A month passed. Ron submitted his completed blueprints, all of which were approved by Larry. There was special praise from Larry for the cobblestone-covered bridge that linked his two estates that Ron had designed. Though short in length, the stone bridge resembled some of the beloved bridges of Paris that connect the left and right banks. It was Ron's distinguished creative mark, the icing on that bordello design cake.

Bridget completed a comprehensive on-site study of interior design, which she did very well in. She continued to take courses as she worked in that field full time.

And Mack? He had a naughty smile on his face as he related a secret that he wanted to tell Ron.

"You must be familiar with the Bible's book of Job, yes, Ron?" he asked.

"Yes, of course. That's where God and the devil decide to test this man named Job. Why do you ask?"

"Larry and I had an ongoing bet on you when you were in Nevada." Mack was smiling as he spoke about the bet.

"What was the bet about?" Ron wanted to find out.

"Larry was so sure that you would not be able to resist the powerful, tempting charms of his girl-friend, Bridget!" He kept smiling. "I told him how strong your love for your family was, and how you can overcome any such temptation," he said and then paused for momentary suspense. "And I won!" Mack tapped Ron's shoulder and then shook his hand, very happy that he had won.

"So, I was your Job?"

"Yes, and I'm so glad I won! If I'd lost I'd be so embarrassed to face Ellen!"

"How much was your money bet?" Ron wanted to know.

"We started with one thousand dollars each, win-ner take all. When Larry thought he was getting the edge, he raised it to five thousand dollars."

The two architects went out for early afternoon drinks to celebrate their victory. Ron recalled the phone conversation that Mack had had that morning before he gave the bordello assignment to him, and how proud he was at getting it. He also recalled those blinding, seductive moments with Bridget. He had fallen deeply for her charms, and Mack could have easily lost his bet. The two very timely phone calls that night got him to see the light, which in turn lit a positive life path for Bridget. It was clear his daughters' prayers had been answered.

The following Sunday, Ron wore his favorite deacon suit for Mass. He walked to the pulpit with his usual quiver of nervousness. When he reached the microphone, he looked in everyone's eyes and then started his sermon. It was the first time the parishioners had heard him raise his baritone voice and also both his arms as he spoke of his own Job experience. He cracked a couple of jokes at well-timed moments, and the parishioners laughed. He was funny. He was eloquent. And just like the cobblestone-covered bridge he had designed for Larry's estate, he was solid, relating, and engaging. Now, he was whole.

TISSUE

The windy rain started at about five in the morning, the same time that early commuters were filling the covered platform to wait for the train. The women had their umbrellas open, ready for the downpour, while the men had their raincoats and hats. The rain was hard and heavy, and everyone was soaked.

Len had his raincoat collar up to cover his neck, his blond hair dripping wet. He stepped on the train just before the door closed and felt relieved that he had made it. He walked the aisle searching for a seat and found one beside a lady who was folding her umbrella. They looked at each other quickly, just as daily commuters do. Their quick impressions of each other were that they were about the same age—early forties—and had the same kind of polite, adapting manner the years of train commuting had taught them. They smiled at each other.

Len took off his wet raincoat, hung it on the arm-rest, and then sat down next to the lady. He took out his handkerchief to wipe his wet hair.

"This is some rain, huh?" he said, and he smiled to be friendly.

"Yes!" she replied and smiled back.

Len's handkerchief was all wet, so he folded it over to find a dry side to wipe his hair again. The lady noticed.

"Would you like a tissue? I have some." She opened her handbag, pulled out a small box of tissues, and offered it to Len, who graciously accepted.

"Thanks," he said as he pulled out a few sheets of the thin, absorbent paper and handed the box back with a smile. "I will *tissue*! Get it? Tissue...tease you?" He was being funny. She laughed; it was a funny pun. The smile on her face remained as she asked him a question.

"Do you work in Manhattan too?" It was her polite way of starting up a commuter conversation with him.

"Yes, I work for DBT Energy downtown. And you?"

"I work for the Cancer Center Hospital."

"Yes, I know where that is. That's near the courthouse?"

"Yes."

"You must be a nurse?"

"Yes, fourteen years in the same hospital." She was proud to say that.

"I went from the courthouse to your hospital cafeteria last week to have lunch there. They have good food there."

"Yes. I'm glad you liked it."

"Just so you know, I was in the courthouse for a divorce-settlement hearing. You don't have to be alarmed."

"Oh, okay," she replied, and they both smiled.

"My name is Len." He offered his moist right hand for a handshake.

"My name is Harriet." She shook his hand.

"Pleased to meet you, Harriet. Thanks for the tissue."

"Did you say you work for DBT Energy?" Harriet asked him.

"Yes, you must have heard about the big fire we had at the upstate plant last month."

"That's why I asked. That was a really big fire!"

"Yes, six employees died," he said and shook his head in sympathy. "I knew them well too."

Their conversation took them to a few more subjects, as each felt the warmth of the other's friendly, pleasant, and focused voice. The train conductor announced their arrival at New York's Penn Station, and the commuters started to get ready. Len and Harriet finished their conversation and then stood up to collect their bags. Both of them found their first conversation nice and interesting and didn't want it to end. That lasting good-naturedness was something Harriet had to tell about to her good friend Gloria, also a nurse on the same floor.

"I will *tissue*! That's what he said to me," Harriet confided to Gloria as she walked into their nurse's station.

"That was funny; you must have laughed!" Gloria agreed.

"Yes, I laughed. I could have laughed even more, but I was being proper," Harriet said.

"Is he good-looking?"

"Respectably good-looking. His hair is starting to thin on top."

"Is he single?"

"Oh, that's another thing I wanted to tell you. He is divorced!" Harriet's face lit up.

"He told you that in your first conversation?" Gloria's eyebrows rose. "Be careful with this guy!"

"Well, at least he was being honest."

The two nurses went about their busy workday at the hospital. Harriet, who was now attuned to that funny use of the word *tissue*, must have heard that word a dozen times in their ward that day. She could not forget Len. Soft-spoken, funny, and divorced. She'd like to meet him again, maybe over dinner.

Harriet had been divorced for four years. Her only son was finishing college in Pennsylvania. Hospital work had become her refuge. A solitary private life, which she had initially dreaded after her divorce, had been quite a blessing. But the need for a special male friend had been a recurring wish, especially when something minor needed to be fixed around the house. Although she had the money to pay for a repairman, the absence of a male chum and confidante had left a desolate void in her life. She lived alone in a quiet house, in which only television conversations were heard. On those lonely days and nights, when her best friends like Gloria were not with her, she yearned for a man to hold and warm up to. She missed the simple caresses of everyday life with a man. Then, suddenly, this fun and witty commuter named Len had appeared in her life. She could forget him.

Len was a recently divorced single parent of two college kids in their early twenties. He and his wife had joint custody, but the kids preferred to live with Len. He was a good cook, and the kids loved that. And as muscular and masculine as he was, Len was also patient, perceptive, and nurturing. These traits came across as unique to anyone meeting him for the first time, as they had to Harriet.

On the train earlier, Harriet had checked him out with admiring side glances. She saw Len as a neat, organized kind of man. She wished she could touch his smooth, clean-shaven jaw, his well-groomed hair, and his striped tie over a light plaid shirt. That handsome, fresh-smelling, cologne-scented guy. It was at this moment that she knew she needed a man in her life. She started to dream of Len, fantasize about him, and hope they would soon reconnect.

Harriet dreamed that Len would one day be admitted to her ward at the hospital. Once there, she would lovingly care for him, feed him, and, during that time, lead him to discover romance with her. But hers was a cancer hospital, she immediately thought. She did not want him to suffer that dreaded disease. Something less serious, something easily curable—appendicitis, perhaps.

"Appendicitis!" Gloria remarked loudly. "You gave him two pieces of tissue, and now he gets appendicitis from you!" Gloria was smiling. "You are one lonely woman, Harriet!" Gloria was her long-time best friend. They had been dorm-mates in nursing college, and they shared and talked about everything, even their dreams of romance.

"I don't know what I was dreaming, Glo. All I know is I want to see him again." Harriet went on her daily commute to and from the city always looking around on the platform and on the train, hoping to catch a glimpse of Len.

Her wish came true one month after their "tissue" meeting. She saw Len seated at the far end of the train car next to a vacant seat. He waved at her to sit with him.

"Hi, Harriet!" She sat next to him and gave him a fake look of surprise.

"Oh, hi. It's Len, right?"

"Yes, good, you remembered."

"What's up?"

"I had an appendectomy!"

"Oh my God! Oh my God!" She was shocked; her face turned pale. She could not believe her dream had come true. "Are you okay?"

"I'm okay now. No need to be alarmed. I was able to rest and relax."

"Oh my God!" she said slowly, as she calmed down. "Where did you get it done? Did somebody take care of you?"

"Yes, my ex-wife took care of me. She was with me for two days."

Harriet kept the smile on her face, not knowing what to say next. The words *appendectomy* and *ex-wife* jolted her back to reality. "Very good!" was all she could say at that awkward moment.

"I have to get off at Woodbridge, Harriet. I have a story assignment here. I'm sure we'll see each other again." He started to get up. He looked at Harriet with an admiring look in his eyes, which met hers squarely.

"I miss you," Len said softly to her ear. Then he got up and walked toward the exit.

"'I miss you!' He told you that? 'I miss you?'" Gloria couldn't believe it.

"Yes, that's what he said before he got off."

"What did you say?"

"I sort of felt annoyed that he had said that."

"I thought you liked him."

"I do, but I didn't know how to react to the words *appendectomy* and *ex-wife*."

"Did you react like you were annoyed?"

"I think I did. I think my face showed some disagreement with the 'I miss you' part."

Suddenly, Gloria's face turned serious; her eyes focused upward as though a lightbulb had just turned on in her brain. She placed her right hand on her forehead as she realized something. "Wait a minute, Harriet, darling. I am beginning to see some kind of pattern with this guy's words."

"Huh?"

"Listen to this. First there was 'I will tissue" and then "I miss you." I think his next words will be "I'll kiss you!" She repeated, "Tissue, miss you, kiss you!"

"Noooo!" Harriet could not see Gloria's prediction coming true.

"I'm pretty sure, Harriet. They all rhyme!"

"But he just told me his ex-wife is back!"

"Back at the hospital when he was sick but maybe not in his life to stay."

"I don't know, Gloria. I don't know if I can kiss a guy with a caring ex-wife; it just does not feel right." Harriet let out a deep sigh of frustration. "We're supposed to be caring nurses, not love-starved divorcees!" Harriet added.

"Maybe, but I want you and your kiss-starved lips to be ready when his very determined lips find yours."

"What will I do if he does?"

"Kiss him back!"

"I don't know if I'm ready to kiss any man back right now."

"Don't lose this guy, Harriet, dear. When that moment comes, close your eyes and kiss him right back! Give him the sweetest, wettest kiss you can give."

Harriet went home with a hopeful, excited smile on her face. The potential kiss was all she could think of. She started daydreaming again. She wondered, Will he kiss me on the train? On the platform, in the rain? Or will he ask me for a date and deliver the kiss in a restaurant? Do I hold back? Or do I give in? She looked at the mirror and tried to rehearse the kissing part. When it happens, if it happens, she has to be ready.

But then she thought, I don't know him that well. Does he have kids? If he does, how old are they? Will we all be good together? There were lots of questions going through her head that kept her up all night. Her alarm clock sounded at 4:30 a.m. Len was still on her mind.

Harriet almost missed the train that morning. She ran as fast as she could, making it just before the doors closed. She saw Len right away; he was looking at her. He waved for her to come sit next to him, and she did.

"I didn't sleep well last night, Harriet. I was thinking of you!" He spoke slowly, nodding his head to punctuate the seriousness of his message. The bags under his eyes showed the lack of sleep.

"Oh?" Harriet answered with a questioning face. Her bags were covered with makeup.

"I want to talk to you, Harriet. Can we get off at the next stop and have coffee and talk? Please, Harriet." He was insistent.

"I'll be late for work."

"Both of us will be late. But this is very important to me!"

"Okay!" She agreed as though she were just being nice to him. But her heart was filled with suspenseful anticipation. She thought of Gloria. Maybe Gloria was right. Maybe the inevitable, glorious kiss would be delivered today wherever the hot coffee was served.

They got off at the Keyport stop. The only places open at that time were 7-Eleven and McDonald's. They got coffee at McDonald's, and then they sat and talked. Len spoke first.

"I said I missed you yesterday, but you did not seem to like that."

"Because you told me your ex-wife was back. So why did you say those words to another woman?"

"My ex-wife is not back in my life; she was just there to be with me at the hospital. You can see I'm not wearing a wedding ring anymore." He showed her both ring-less hands. Then Len said, "I know you're divorced too!" He looked at her for the truth, but his remark brought a scowl to her face.

"How did you know that? I still have my ring!" She was a bit indignant.

"I don't think you would be having coffee with me early in the morning if you were married," Len said in a very soft voice, almost apologizing for the idea.

He's right, Harriet thought. Her marital status was no secret anymore. Len continued. "I said I missed you because I really, really did miss you, Harriet. I have to tell you the words that are in my heart." He did not want to stop talking. "Let me tell you something about me, Harriet." He paused to swallow and then continued. "Do you remember the big fire at our power plant last month?

"Yes," Harriet responded.

"Remember when our CEO read his statement on the news?

"Yes, I remember."

"I was the one who wrote that statement. I am a public-relations writer. I had crafted that statement with words that evaded the truth." He paused to take a deep breath. "We were not supposed to admit fault because it would affect our insurance claims. We were not supposed to say anything that would give any clue of our negligence to the fire investigators." He paused for another moment. "Our CEO spoke for about half an hour, saying the words that I wrote and sounding very apologetic. But all of it meant nothing at all. The only true words he said were when he expressed his sympathy for those who died. That was truly a tragic loss." He stopped and sipped his steaming coffee.

"Why are you telling me this, Len?" Harriet asked.

"Because I can tell you that I love you in so many words and so many phrases, but I prefer to be honest with you with just a few carefully chosen and meaningful words; words that are coming honestly from my heart." Len looked at Harriet intently and then continued. "Harriet, when I was in the hospital, I was praying that you would be the nurse caring for me and feeding me and that your pretty face would be looking at me."

Harriet recalled that that had been her wish too. She could feel the sincerity of Len's words. Now, she could feel she was falling in love. But there was one big question she had to have answered.

"What about your ex-wife?"

"Yes, she was there to care for me, but you were the one and only person on my mind." He paused. "That was when I truly, truly missed you."

Harriet felt enlightened and relieved. Len's honest words had answered most of the questions that had crowded her mind, making way for a new beginning in their lives. All other issues would be sorted out later. They held hands at the table and looked at each other without saying a word. Then Len leaned forward, as though he wanted to tell her something. Could this be the kiss moment? She thought. Instinctively, she closed her eyes, primed her lips, and leaned forward toward him as well.

"Can I squeeze you?" Len whispered softly yet passionately to Harriet's ear.

Harriet broke into loud, hearty laughter when she heard those words. *Tissue, miss you,* and *squeeze you.* She couldn't stop laughing. All her anxieties and unease had been lifted. Those might not have been the words she was waiting dearly to hear from Len at that moment, but, short and witty, they were the finest words of genuine male affection she had heard in a long time.

WO AI NI

Porfirio Soarez Torre was a Spanish-Portuguese-American car salesman. He would congenially introduce himself using his nickname, Roy, but his friends called him Suave, and for good reason. He was smooth, glib, and persuasive in most everything he did, especially when he was selling cars and enticing women to fall in love with him. For most of his adult life, Suave had been an award-winning, quota-busting car salesman and, at the same time, an amorous, passionate, romantic gigolo.

"I fall in love so easily," he would tell his closest friends, who would enviously probe him for his adventures (and sometimes misadventures) with women. "And they fall in love so easily with me too!" Suave would add. He had been quick to spot the lonely, needy women—the widows, the jilted, the neglected. Almost effortlessly, his confident charm would gently tame their resistance, and they would fall head over heels for him. They would find in him the comfort of love and companionship and a fun, satisfying physical experience, until he finds another woman he wants to pursue.

Suave had grown up in the rough, blue-collar, Portuguese section of Newark, New Jersey, the big city across the Hudson River from New York City. Newark was where silky cherry blossoms flourished in early spring, but where crime statistics showed a much truer picture of life in the city. His father had worked for a men's haberdasher, where Suave had learned how to dress up and dress well. His mother had been a pleasant, sought-after beautician who did home service, going to women's homes to do their makeup, manicures, and pedicures. She had often been accompanied by young Roy when they could not find a sitter for him. It was during his mother's home-service rounds that Suave had learned of both the loveliness and ugliness of the female mood and spirit. It was an education that served him well professionally and in his relationships with women but not when dealing with their jealous husbands and boyfriends.

When he was seventeen, Suave had had an intimate romance with his high school's homecoming queen, whose boyfriend had been a college football athlete. The whole football team had come out to hunt for Suave. And Suave would never forget the wealthy businessman husband of a thirty-two-year-old mother of two. The husband had come to Suave's house with two muscled thugs holding baseball bats, looking to avenge his wife's affair with Suave, who was only nineteen at the time. Suave had jumped out the back window and ran away. But instead of learning the painful lessons that came with these affairs, Suave had done what he thought he needed to do. He'd lifted weights at the gym, started to train for the marathon, and studied Tae kwon do.

Two years of faithful commitment to the gym had transformed his physique into a muscled, alert runner, which had complemented his handsome face. He was even more handsome then and more eye-catching to women. And more than ever, he had struck boldly at women because he was able to face the physical challenges from their jealous men. Most men would think it to be quite an exciting, amorous adventure of a life, but Suave didn't. Not anymore.

Suave was now sixty-two years old, living alone in his low-rent studio apartment in Newark, enduring the pains of arthritis in his hands and arms, and subsisting on his meager Social-Security pension. He had been married twice to well-educated, professional women with whom he had had two children each. Suave had a total of seven children from both inside and outside his marriages. None of his past lovers and none of his children will have anything to do with him now. So, even with the approximately thirty lovers he'd had in his life, today he lives alone in his run-down apartment. No friends to talk to, no one to greet him with "Happy Birthday, Suave!"

For his birthday, he had gone to his favorite Chinese restaurant and ordered shrimp lo mein. And it never fails: the memory of a young, pretty, Chinese waitress named Jiah would come to mind whenever he had Chinese food. Jiah was then twenty-three years old. Suave had been thirty-nine and newly divorced from his second wife.

To Suave, Jiah had the sweetest, loveliest, reserved face at the Sapphire Chinese Buffet, where she'd worked as a waitress. Of all the Asian-looking faces that had served in that restaurant, Jiah's face had stood out for Suave. Unlike the curt, sometimes mildly rude waitresses, Jiah had been a gracious and attentive server since the first time he'd eaten there. Right away, Suave had been smitten. He'd been so smitten by this Asian beauty, her skin so soft and flawlessly smooth, like well-crafted porcelain, that he repeatedly ate there, sometimes as many as five times a week, always leaving her good tips to impress her and chatting with her as they discovered each other.

Suave had learned that Jiah had grown up in the town of Changsha, the capital of Hunan Province in south central China. It was in Changsha that the young Mao Tse-Tung, who became the powerful party leader, had first been introduced to communism. Jiah's father was a factory worker who strived hard to feed his wife and four children. Jiah was the eldest. Three years before Jiah and Suave had met, she had been offered work in this Woodbridge, New Jersey, restaurant just as she graduated from high school. Without any hesitation, she'd packed her few pieces of clothing and tearfully said good-bye to the family she dearly loved, all of them wishing she would someday find the good fortune her good heart had always dreamed of.

Naïveté, honesty, and innocence. These were the qualities that had lured the worldly Suave to Jiah. She had felt so sorry for Suave about his bitter divorce. Suave, who'd felt quite lost at that time, had seen Jiah's sympathy for him as the perfect pathway to this equally lonely Chinese girl's heart. One evening, as Jiah had poured hot tea into his ceramic cup, Suave had caressed her hand, and they had fallen in love.

Wo ai ni means "I love you" in Mandarin, and those were some of the few words the couple had intimately reserved for each other. They had had a blissful romantic involvement and had both looked toward a lasting, committed relationship.

Wo ai ni became very special words for Suave. After the many casual and indifferent relationships he'd had with women, he'd thought Jiah might be the woman who would put his amorous cravings to an end. He was, after all, getting older.

And so the two dated. Suave had amazed Jiah by taking her on road trips in his 2005 Mustang convertible, and she in turn had cooked the delicious Chinese dishes that he had come to savor. There was this noodle dish that Jiah had invented just for them, the "JiaSu red beets lo mein." It was noodles cooked in shrimp stock with midsize shrimp and green vegetables made colorful with red beets. The red beets stood out in this dish as a symbol of their intense love for each other. Jiah had explained to Suave that the long strands of noodles symbolized long life in Asian lore—a bit of wisdom that Suave had kept in mind. They had been very happy. So happy that Suave had said to himself, "She is it. Jiah is the last girl I will love. I will marry her, and my gigolo days are over. I want to settle down, raise a family with her, and keep this happy relationship for the rest of my life." They continued dating.

Freedom and independence are the life pursuits that gigolos always value. Suave had not cared to do the fatherly duties of helping with homework, taking kids to the dentist, doing yard work, and paying school tuition. But Suave looked forward to doing all that with Jiah and to staying happy with her. There was, however, her need for a green card.

The US Immigration and Naturalization Service can be overbearing in a couple's life due to the many requirements of this government office. The agency checked if Suave was regularly paying child support, which he was not. As soon as Suave had felt the burden of said requirements, their dating days had become less frequent, until they had finally come to a full stop. Suave had been frustrated. As much as he loved Jiah, Suave had wanted out.

The separation had been crushing for the lovers. Suave had once again drifted into the arms of other women, while Jiah had gone back to work at Sapphire Chinese Buffet. After about a year apart, Suave had gone to the restaurant one day and found that Jiah no longer worked there. He'd learned that she had gone to Seattle to be with her sister. It was the end of this love affair, yet another failed affair, for love-seeking, love-starved Suave, who'd plunged into his wicked gigolo lifestyle once more. There would be one more failed marriage for Suave, his third. After that, he grew lonelier and much more withdrawn.

On this sixty-second birthday meal, as he skillfully worked his chopsticks on his plate of his shrimp lo mein at the Chinese restaurant, Suave recalled the folklore wisdom regarding noodles that Jiah had once taught him. Noodles symbolized long life. Suave tried to apply the meaning of that folklore to his life today. While his body remained fairly healthy, his solitary existence had allowed him much time for quiet, penitent reflection. He missed Jiah dearly. He was convinced of that.

It had been about twenty years since his love affair with Jiah. He recalled how he had caressed her flawlessly smooth skin. He remembered her shiny, dark hair, her shy smile, and then her painful tears when he'd broken off their affair. How did she manage after that? He wondered now. It did not take long before he mustered the resolve to set things right.

"I have to find her!" Suave vowed to himself. "I need Jiah now, and I must win her back!" Suave felt a surge of intense love for Jiah, the Chinese girl who'd shared with him the truest, most honest love he had ever had with a woman in his life. He set out to find her.

Suave made a list of all the Chinese restaurants in Seattle and called each one of them asking for a woman named Jiah. After calling about nine restaurants, he heard one promising reply.

"Jiah busy now. Call back three p.m." Then he heard the click of the receiver.

Suave's heart was pounding with excitement. He started thinking of the right words to say to Jiah. He wrote them down. He would tell Jiah that he was deeply sorry for leaving her, that he was wrong and stupid for doing that, that he would understand perfectly if she hated him today, that he was all alone at the moment, and that he loves her and never stopped loving her. *Wo ai ni.* He must not forget to utter those very crucial words of love to her. And he prayed as he had never prayed before.

Suave got up and ran towards a Catholic church about a mile from his apartment. *Wo ai ni.* The words repeated themselves in his desperate mind as he ran, praying that Jiah would take him back. It was almost two o'clock when Suave opened the heavy church door, gasping and trying to catch his breath. He knelt at the first pew. As he prayed, he heard the whispers of voices inside the confessional box. He decided to line up for confession.

"Bless me, Father, for I have sinned. I cannot remember my last confession."

"Unload your burdens to me, my son. Tell me your sins, and don't hold back!" Suave was encouraged by the priest's opening response. It was a distinct, mellow, baritone voice from the other side of the wicker wall. Suave could see a male priest with salt-and-pepper hair and a trimmed beard. As the priest had encouraged him to do, Suave unloaded and did not hold back. He confessed all his sins with all the women he'd ever loved and had intimate relationships with.

"Okay, okay! I get the picture, my son!" The priest stopped Suave from going on. "Let me ask you, my son—what made you come here for confession today?"

Suave had to stop and think. "I was eating shrimp lo mein, and I remembered Jiah. I always remember her whenever I eat Chinese noodles, Father!"

"You're making me hungry. I love shrimp lo mein too. I did missionary work in Taipei for eight years."

Suave excitedly proceeded to tell the priest of their JiaSu red beets lo mein. The priest gave him a quick, meaningful education on regional food.

"You must have been a very special man to this woman, my son." The priest paused to look at Suave through the wicker wall. "Did you know that red beets are rare root crops in China where I was? They only serve red beets at special events or on special occasions."

It was like a solid punch to Suave's face. How insensitive he had been to Jiah's true love! She had not been too good with English words, but she had conveyed her love for him through her cooking, a craft that she knew so well. Suave started to stand up, wanting more than ever to hear Jiah's voice. But the priest was not finished with him.

"For your penance, you have to pray the rosary every day for one week. God bless you, my son. I hope you get a second chance with this woman that you love!" Suave made the sign of the cross when he saw the priest give him his blessing. He left the church hurriedly and ran back to his apartment, all the while praying that Jiah would find it in her heart to forgive him.

It was exactly 3:00 p.m. Seattle time when Suave dialed the number. A female voice answered after three rings.

"Wok D Wok!" She had the Chinese accent.

"Jiah!" Suave was filled with anxiety.

"My name is Sia, not Jiah."

"Is Jiah there?" His heart was pounding.

"No, Jiah no work here."

"Do you know where I can call her?" Suave was getting frustrated.

"Jiah moved to Bellevue; I don't know where." Click. She hung up.

Suave was undeterred. He started calling restaurants in the Seattle suburb of Bellevue. Patiently, he dialed the numbers, speaking as slowly and clearly as he could and hoping to get a reliable response and some helpful information. Then he heard that familiar, soft, sweet voice—the loveliest voice on earth for Suave at that moment—and his heart stood still.

"Lotus Charm Buffet!"

"Jiah?"

"Who's this?"

"It's Suave; do you remember me?"

There was a few seconds of silence from her end, then she responded, saying simply, "Hi." She could barely be heard due to the customers' noise.

Suave's search was over. He had found his sweetest love, Jiah, the love of his life. He started to say the words he had long wanted to say to her from his heart. He sputtered at the start.

"Jiah, I am so sorry. I hope you can forgive me!" His voice started to crack. He was about to start his next sentence when Jiah cut him off.

"Do you want to order, sir?" Her voice was stern and businesslike.

With a sorry tone in his voice, Suave said, "I just want to talk to you briefly!"

"Please call back with your order, sir." Click.

Suave sat on his bed, able to understand the honest anger that Jiah had vented to him over the phone. He deserved it. He deserved the rude treatment. But he thanked God anyway that he'd finally found her. Right away he decided that he was going to fly to Bellevue, on the other side of the country, to see his lovely Jiah face-to-face, to tell her he still loved her, and to convince her to love him back.

As impulsive a decision as it was, Suave gathered all the money he had and ran to the nearest jewelry store to buy an engagement ring for Jiah. He prayed she would accept it. Then he packed a small weekender bag and booked the first flight to Seattle-Tacoma International Airport. He knew it was going to be a long, bumpy flight. In his mind, he explored all the possible rendezvous scenarios he might have with Jiah. His mind was filled with what-ifs. What if she's married? He thought. No problem. He would just talk to her and tell her how sorry he continues to be to this day. Then he would fly back and not bother her again. What if she's not married? He thought about that next, and that thought brought a smile to his lips. He would again woo her, "bring spring to her, and long for the days when he'll cling to her," just as the song lyrics go. He was in a light, amorous mood as he hummed the lovely tune.

It was about four in the afternoon when the taxi brought Suave to the Lotus Charm Buffet in Bellevue, Washington. Near the restaurant he noticed a light-rail train stop where commuters were boarding. It was clean, gleaming, and well planned, much like the rest of Bellevue. He was impressed.

He could not help but take slower steps as he walked toward the restaurant door. He was nervous. It was summertime so he wore a blue-striped, short-sleeved dress shirt with a matching necktie, the garb Jiah would be expecting him to wear on this pleasantly warm afternoon. He looked around trying to find that beautiful, flawless face, but he didn't see her. He sat at a booth and ordered tea. The waitress smiled and told him he could go ahead and get his food from the buffet tables. His heart was about to burst as he asked the waitress, "Is Jiah here?"

"She's in the kitchen, but she'll be out soon." The waitress went off to get his tea. He was tense and fidgety, tapping his fingers on the table as he waited.

He was about to stand up and get some appetizers when he heard the voice he'd been longing to hear.

"Hi, Suave!" He turned around and there she was, wearing a light-green silk cheongsam. The Jiah of his dreams.

"God, you're beautiful, Jiah!" He was astonished at how stunningly beautiful she was, and as she smiled at him, she was even more beautiful.

"You gained some weight, Suave!" she replied as she likewise looked at him from head to toe.

"A little bit," he replied. "Can you join me for dinner, Jiah?"

"No, I can't. Employees are not allowed to sit with customers."

"I noticed you're not wearing the employees' uniform. You must be the manager now?"

"My husband and I own this restaurant, Suave." She said that as if to brag. She was not about to talk idly, either; she had to ask the big question.

"Why did you come here, Suave?"

"I wanted to see you and talk to you, Jiah. You wouldn't talk to me on the phone."

"I was really hurt when you broke up with me!" she said. Her face and eyes got serious.

"That's the main reason I came. I wanted to tell you that I am so sorry, and I hope you will forgive me, Jiah." His right hand was on his chest, and his face showed much remorse.

"After twenty years, Suave, you felt sorry for me?" She was unmoved.

"Again, Jiah, I am so sorry. You might not believe this, but I always think of you, most especially when I eat Chinese food." He bowed his head slightly to admit some shame, saying, "I also wanted to see how you are doing now. I see that you are doing well here in Bellevue."

"We own five restaurants now, Suave, all in this part of the state." She had that modest bragging tone again.

"Wow, Jiah, that's very good!" He was really impressed.

"And I want to thank you, Suave. You indirectly contributed to my success." She smiled.

"Really, Jiah? How?"

"When we broke up, I vowed never to be poor and helpless again. So I learned English and went to business school."

"Yes, I noticed your English is very, very good."

"That was where I met my husband, Scott. He is second-generation Chinese. He's a very smart businessman." Again with that modest bragging tone.

"Do you have children?"

"We have a daughter who's graduating from medical school!" Jiah was obviously quite proud of her family. Just as she finished speaking, a short, stocky, Chinese man wearing a white shirt and yellow tie walked over to Jiah. It was her husband.

"Scott, this is Mr. Suave. He used to be our customer in New Jersey." Suave stood up to shake Scott's hand.

"How are you, Mr. Suave? What brings you to Bellevue?"

"Oh, just visiting some old friends from New Jersey," he lied.

"Enjoy your visit, Mr. Suave!" Scott said and then turned to Jiah. "I have to go to the South Street restaurant, hon. I'll see you later."

"*Wo ai ni*," Jiah said, and she smiled as she kissed her husband. Suave thought she said the words a bit louder so he may surely hear.

"*Wo ai ni*, hon!" her husband replied, as he kissed her back and hurriedly walked out.

The sight of Jiah kissing her husband was like a sharp dagger that tore through Suave's heart. It was now Suave having to accept and bear the pain of rejection instead of all the women he had dumped in the past. And he should be the one saying "*Wo ai ni*" to Jiah, not Scott. That was another punch in the face for Suave. He kept the hurting, fake smile as Scott headed for the door.

Jiah looked in the direction of the door and waited until her husband exited. Then she looked at Suave. "You haven't told me about you, Suave. How are you doing now?"

He spoke of how he felt. "I still love you, Jiah!" This time, his smile faded, and he felt a bitter lump in his throat right after saying it.

"You're too late, Suave. I am now a happily married woman!"

Suave heaved a deep sigh of disappointment; he could hardly contain his tears. "I could see that, Jiah, but I just wanted you to know that I will always love you." Suave stood up from his chair and straightened his tie to get ready to leave.

Jiah stopped him, saying, "Wait, Suave. I asked the cook to wrap some food for you to eat at the hotel." She waved her hand to the cook, who was waiting nearby with a white take-out pack. Right away, Suave smelled the aroma of shrimp, noodles, and beef stock. He looked at Jiah, who was smiling back at him. He decided to open the take-out pack immediately. When he did, he saw that there were no red beets on top of the noodles. None. He looked back at Jiah, whose eyes had a look of revenge that ended any hope of getting back together. "*Wo ai ni,* Jiah," he whispered to her, a final futile attempt to express his deep feelings. Then Suave walked out.

Until we lose something, we never know its value. Suave now had to head back to an empty apartment to be alone with just his memories of what he used to believe was gigolo fun. One by one, he thought of the women who could have shared his empty rooms with him. None of them were with him today. Gigolo Suave had had the love of so many women who'd begged him to love them back. But he had recklessly squandered all that love until there was no more left.

Suave walked eastward, where he saw the light-rail commuters gathering at the train station. He kept walking, taking slow, heavy steps, farther from the station but closer to the tracks. When he was about ten yards away from the waiting crowd, he stopped and examined the tracks in front of him. He heard the sound of the bell signaling the arriving train. The commuters moved about settling themselves on the platform, guessing where the doors might conveniently open for them. Suave did not move. He took out the engagement ring from his pocket, threw the box away, and placed the ring in his mouth. He then closed his eyes, gathered enough saliva in his mouth, and swallowed the precious gem. He faced the bright headlight coming around the bend. The train was slowing down. As the train dragged closer to him, he walked closer to the tracks. Determined to end it all, he stood in the train's path.

The engineer saw a man on the tracks, just a few feet away, and instinctively hit the brakes. But it was too late. The man was run over by the unforgiving metal wheels of the train. The crew quickly rushed down to check on him as the crowd gathered around, desperately hoping the man was still alive. They saw the take-out pack of Chinese noodles by his side, still warm. An older lady who had witnessed the whole incident had shakenly recounted the events, saying, "His hands were both raised up, and I heard him shouting, **'Woe eye knee! Woe eye knee!'** He yelled it a few times." She paused to catch her breath. "Those words did not make any sense to me." Her face was pale from shock at the sudden death she had seen.

Shaking his head in disbelief as he knelt to examine the bloody, mangled body of Suave, the train conductor very curiously asked, "You said you heard him shout 'Woe eye knee?'"

"Yes, that's what I heard. Woe eye knee. The words did not make any sense!"

"He must have been a doctor, or a therapist," the conductor hastily concluded.

Arguably, given the comfort and companionship Suave romantically provided to the many women in his life, in a way we can say he was a therapist.

SCHOOL OF
ECONOMICS

The auditorium was packed at New York University's Stern School of Business. The crowd, mostly college students with some gray-haired, well-dressed professors mixed in, mingled as they waited. There were about a dozen male guests wearing green New York City sanitation department uniforms who sat close to each other at the rear of the auditorium and seemed a bit hesitant to mingle. They were seen chatting and laughing with the well-dressed men who were to speak that evening.

There were four speakers listed. All were African American men around sixty-five years old. One of them was in a wheelchair. The other three men looked agile and healthy as they made their entrance onto the stage. At 7:10 p.m., the young emcee started the symposium.

"Good evening, and welcome to our quarterly business symposium here at NYU's Stern School of Business. The goal of this symposium is to invite successful entrepreneurs to speak about the ideas, hard work, decisions, and other essentials that made them rise and succeed in business. As students of business, we can all learn from them. My name is Robert Macaraig, and I am a senior in NYU's masters of business administration program." He pulled out a small piece of yellow paper from his coat pocket. Going through his list, he continued.

"I came across this car dealer when I lived at the Jersey shore last summer. My uncle, who lives there, asked me to stay at their house while they went home to the Philippines for a vacation. Instead of taking the bus, I learned that there was a car dealer near my uncle's house that had commuter passenger vans going to New York City. That was when I met these four gentlemen, who were nice enough to be here with us tonight." The emcee pointed to the four men and then went on. "Their story is one of old-school funds management, innovative marketing, clever foresight, and bold decision-making being the keys to their tremendous success. When I heard their business story, I could not sleep. I knew I had to bring them here to you to share their incredible story. If I were to create a title for their story, I'd call it "The Sewer School of Economics" or, better yet, "Unlocking Caged Dreams." He paused and then continued.

"I will let them tell their story to you now," Robert said as he turned to look at the man nearest the microphone. "Here now is their unofficial spokesman, Mr. William Bell." A tall African American man with medium build and graying hair stood up from the panel table and walked toward the podium amid loud applause. He was wearing a dark-blue suit, white shirt, and purple-striped tie, and he carried a smile of pride and the dignity of hard-earned success. He was a little nervous at the start.

"Good evening, students and faculty and guests of NYU's Stern School of Business. My name is William Bell, but you can all call me Billy. I am here with my business partners, Abe, Teddy, and Paul Jr. We want to thank your emcee, Robert, for inviting us to speak to you tonight." He then turned to look at the emcee.

"I like that title, 'The Sewer School of Economics,' Rob!" He then looked at the audience. "Robert is a very smart, very curious young man, especially on business matters. We all enjoyed his probing questions and his likeable company. He even took us to his uncle's house for Filipino food by the pool." Everybody laughed and applauded, and Billy continued. "Folks, if you haven't tasted Filipino food yet, and we hadn't until Robert appeared in our lives, it is the most delicious food on all the earth! My mouth is craving the spring rolls, the pancit, and adobo," he said as he folded his fingers to kiss them. There was loud applause, and even louder applause from the sanitation group. Billy then turned serious.

"I believe the one thing that intrigued Robert about our story is the fact that all four of us worked for the sanitation department in New York City's sewer system." The audience was silent.

"Yes, before we had this car dealership, we worked at the sewer, the largest sewer network system in the world." He paused, and the audience remained silent.

"And it was there in the underground sewer system, amid the filth and stench of it all, that we envisioned and planned our business." Some in the audience took a deep breath as they waited for Billy to narrate the amazing story.

"Ours is not a rags-to-riches story. We all felt blessed that we had fairly good-paying jobs at the sanitation department. But working in the sewer for years will make one think, is this the only job for me? Is there anything else I can do to make a decent living? All four of us tried to look for jobs outside the sewer system but were unsuccessful.

"Our business story started one day when I had a job interview at a restaurant in Manhattan. After working in the sewer for three years, I tried to apply for a job as a waiter. I can still remember the look on the manager's face when she saw on my application that I was working in the sewer. She could not hide the look of disgust on her face. It was like she could smell the stench and filth of the sewer on me." He stopped to clear his throat. "She said they would call me, and I waited for their call, but it never came." The room remained silent, everyone listening to Billy's every word.

"From then on, we knew we had to keep working in the sewer. The pay was not bad, and we decided to save money." He then pointed to the man in the wheelchair. "Abe was the one who convinced us that we had to save our money so we could start our own business someday. So every week on payday, all four of us would give him ten dollars for our business fund." Billy walked toward the guy in the wheelchair, placed his right hand proudly on his shoulder, and continued.

"This guy, Abe, my friends, is the best financial mind I know. He could have been a top notch CPA if he had only had the chance. He accounted for every penny of our savings fund, making sure it yielded the best interest rate. He will now tell you his story and his role in the business." The audience applauded. Billy walked to the back of Abe's wheelchair and pushed it gently toward the microphone. He then adjusted it lower for Abe, who started to speak.

"Hello, faculty and students and guests. My name is Abe Bloom. I started out as, and still am, this gang's treasurer," he said, as mild laughter came from the audience. "My father worked in the sewer. My father's early death from cancer did not allow me to study further. I was able to finish high school, though, and I was the only one of the four of us who did. My job in the sewer saved me from a dark life on the mean streets of New York City. Our jobs underneath the streets saved all four of us from the clutches of drugs and violent gangs. Why?" He pointed to the other three to emphasize. "Because the four of us had great, big ideas that were made even larger by our work inside those underground sewer pipes that we knew we would be free from someday!" There was mild applause.

"I was the one who suggested to the gang that every month we should go to the Jersey shore to inhale the fresh ocean air so it could clean our lungs, and our minds. And we did, sometimes twice a month. We would take the train from Penn Station straight to the shores of Asbury Park, Belmar, Avon, Bradley Beach, and Point Pleasant Beach. And there we would talk about our business ideas, lots of ideas. We loved those weekends at the Jersey shore so much that we all decided to settle there. In 1999, when interest rates dropped dramatically, we all decided to move there." The audience stayed silent, listening intently.

"Of all the business ideas we brainstormed about, there was one that persisted despite being set aside so often." He then pointed to Paul Jr., who was seated at the end of the table. "That guy kept bringing up this idea. Here to talk about it is our very own Paul Campbell Jr." The audience applauded the youthful-looking man, who stood up and walked to the microphone. He was the shortest of the group, about five feet seven, with a trim waist and muscular build. His hands looked very much like the muscular hands of a weightlifter. In a soft, low-decibel voice, he enlightened everyone on his business idea.

"Good evening. My name is Paul Campbell Jr., you may call me Junior. I worked as a mechanic at the sanitation department motor pool." He paused to take a deep breath; he was obviously nervous.

"There were a lot of business ideas that we discussed. We thought of putting up a restaurant, a dollar store, a 7-Eleven, and a retail gun store. Yes, a gun store." His face turned serious. He took a deep breath and continued.

"As you know, ladies and gentlemen, gun sales go up whenever we get news of mass shootings." He paused. "Guns, my friends, practically sell themselves! There is a lot of money to be made selling guns." His voice was becoming louder. "We had very emotional arguments about guns. In fact, we fought over this product. It was during those arguments that some of the deadliest mass shootings happened."

He paused a bit longer. "We then realized that as dark as it was in the sewer, selling guns was an even darker and deadlier kind of business. Nothing in it was pleasant, fair, or optimistic," he explained. "We realized that if we sold a gun to a customer for self-defense, there would be a good chance that the gun would carelessly fall into the wrong hands and accidentally kill someone, even possibly the customer who bought it." Junior looked at the audience.

"Ladies and gentlemen, the gun business is not who we are!" The audience was likewise divided; those who opposed guns cheered, while those in favor of guns kept politely silent and looked at each other, rolling their eyes and sneering. He stopped to take a drink. It was clear that he got emotional over the subject. Then he continued.

"What I suggested was a passenger-van commuting service that took New Jersey commuters to their workplaces in New York City in the morning and brought them back in the evening. I am very familiar with repairing twelve-seater vans because we worked on them at the motor pool. That was the idea that seemed to gain traction at our discussions. I was also very persistent and very confident in my mechanic skills." Junior had come to the story of the start of their business, and the audience remained attentive.

"All of us started work at the sewer at about the same time. We all took early retirement at age sixty-two. We all had fairly good pensions and Social Security, and, don't forget, while at work we continued to save money. We saved ten dollars a week at first, but later we raised it to twenty." He paused to clear his throat.

"We had saved close to twenty-seven thousand dollars by the time we retired. That became the seed money for our business." Knowing he was going to give specifics on the money, he paused to take a drink from a water bottle. Then he continued.

"We bought a used fifteen-passenger commuter van from a Presbyterian church for seven thousand dollars. It was a 2005 GMC Savana, a van that I knew quite well. It had a hundred thirty thousand miles on it." He paused.

"And, as expected, I replaced all the old belts and hoses, replaced the radiator, and did all the other needed repair work. Meanwhile, my buddies reupholstered and repainted it, until it smelled like brand new. Altogether, we spent about six thousand for repairs and cleaning. Then, we were in business." He paused to take a deep breath. "We named the business Four Folks Shuttle." The audience applauded at the name; they could see the four friends in their first van, riding in it and facing an uncertain business future. Junior continued.

"Finding commuters from the Jersey shore to New York City was easy. In fact, we had so many that we had to keep a waiting list. All four of us took turns driving. It was the start of more business ideas." He then pointed to the remaining man on the panel who had not yet spoken. "Teddy had some great ideas for the commuter van business. Here now is our good friend, Teddy Washington." The audience was feeling the suspense. They wanted to know more, so they applauded wildly for Teddy, who stood up and walked to the microphone as Junior sat down. Teddy was thin and graceful, with good bearing on clothes.

"Good evening. My name is Teddy Washington. Working within the confines of the sewer made me imagine lots of business ideas. Most of them came out when we started the commuter van business." He then went straight to his ideas.

"The passenger transport van is very efficient. The van is smaller than a bus, so it can weave through the lanes more easily and cut travel time by about half an hour. But before we even had our first commuter van, I had a question." He paused. "What were we going to do with the return trip from New York?" He put his right finger to his head. "Were we just going to allow the van to travel back empty? That seemed like a waste of gas to me. We didn't want to park the van in New York all day either, because parking is expensive. Besides, the driver for that morning trip would be tired if he waited there all day. The driver has a very early start in the morning, and he needs to rest at midday." He paused, still pointing to his head. He explained his new idea.

"What I did was, I tried to find businesses in New York and New Jersey that would want to courier or deliver their goods to their customers across the tunnel. I found them, and there were a lot of them." He then explained his plan. "So, after unloading the passengers in New York City in the morning, our drivers would go to businesses and pick up cargo, such as Thai glutinous rice, Chinese century eggs, Madras curry, and Philippine fish sauce. We charged less than the truckers." He paused to take a deep breath. He was excited to narrate his business idea. He continued.

"On the way back in the afternoon, our van would be loaded with goods from Jersey, such as pizza boxes, eggplants, pharmaceutical products, and much more." He stopped when he saw a raised hand for a question.

"Don't those things smell in the van?" one student asked.

"Yes, they do. Oh, yes they do," he said as he started to laugh. "Especially the fish sauce and curry. But remember, there are four of us. Once the goods are delivered, we give the van a nice, thorough cleaning to make sure there are no unwelcome smells for our commuters." Another hand was raised.

"What happens when the van breaks down on the road?"

Junior stood up to answer. "We make sure the vans are in good shape to prevent breakdowns, but of course they still happen. We have an agreement with the local auto-rental companies that allows us to rent their vans for our emergencies." The audience liked the rehearsed narrative. Teddy continued as Junior sat down.

"There is another part of our business that I thought about, and that is our concierge service. Yes, our very own concierge service." He smiled proudly when he uttered the French word. "What we did was, we put together a list of services that our customers would want us to do for them during the day, and they would get them when they came back at night. But what kinds of services would we offer?" He smiled again as he posed that question.

"For example, on their way back from work in New York City, they want their clothes dry-cleaned. Remember, those New York customers dress up well to go to work. Or they want flowers for their spouses, bottles of wine and liquor, buckets of hot Kentucky Fried Chicken, even a two-piece bathing suit for a girlfriend." The audience laughed. "For a fee, all these would be waiting for them when they get back." He paused. "That was how our business progressed," Teddy said, winding up his part. He then looked at Billy, who stood up. "Now I'd like to give you back to Billy," Teddy said, and he went back to his seat as Billy walked to the microphone.

"For two years, we did our business that way. We had our van commuters, our courier delivery services, and our concierge services." He smiled proudly. "Let me tell you, folks, business was very good, because in two years, we needed two more brand-new vans. And we bought them!" The audience applauded loudly.

"In our third year, one of our commuters spoke to me while I was driving the van and said she wanted to buy a car. She told me that she had had very bad experiences with buying cars and that the salespeople intimidated her. So she asked me to negotiate a deal for her to buy a Toyota RAV4." Billy waited a couple of minutes to allow some suspense to build. The audience stayed silent, and he continued.

"It just so happened that the two vans we had bought recently were Toyotas, so I went to see my salesman and his manager and asked for a good deal on the RAV4. And we got her a great deal, so good she could not believe it!" The audience applauded. Billy waited for the room to quiet down, and then he continued.

"That was when we seriously discussed setting up a car dealership. We knew we had the very vital trust of our commuters. We had always kept good relationships with them, and they were growing in number. They turned out to be our future car buyers. At that time, we had five commuter vans, and we needed more." Billy paused for a moment and then went on.

"We found a nice-sized piece of land on a busy stretch of Route 35. It had an old, run-down restaurant building on it. It was mired in a few lawsuits, but luckily the principal owners had passed and the heirs were now willing to negotiate to sell it. That was good timing for us. So Abe and I negotiated with our bank and the auto companies. It was the Ford Motor Company that was willing to give us a chance at having our dealership. We wanted a Japanese carmaker also, but Ford did not want a mixed dealership where two car brands would compete with each other on the same lot." Billy stopped to look at his three friends, who nodded to him. He was about to start a crucial part of their story.

"We found another property that was for sale on the same street. It was on the other side, about two thousand feet north of the first one. This property had a deeper space in the rear, which we needed for our commuter parking. They were willing to give us a good deal too. We were all excited." He paused and then continued.

"The whole package was to be a loan for sixty-five million dollars. We didn't have that much money. Our bank did not have that kind of money either; they wanted to cover only a third of that." Billy's voice became sparse. He began speaking in intervals because he was getting emotional. "It was also at this time that Abe suffered a stroke." Billy stopped as he felt a big lump in his throat. He could not go on. He paused to drink from his water bottle again, still unable to speak. He must have recounted this story many times before, but this time he felt a tide of emotions. Abe wheeled himself to the microphone to continue. The two friends shook hands, and then Billy went back to his seat. Abe started to speak.

"Billy always gets emotional when he shares this part of our business story. I just want to continue." He paused and then said, "Yes, I had a stroke, and a very bad one too. Half of my body felt numb, my face was deformed, and I was in a comatose state for two weeks. All the property and dealership negotiations were put on hold. The three of them had second thoughts about the deal. They were thinking that my stroke was a sign that we shouldn't go through with it." Everyone in the audience was waiting for the story to continue.

The sound of a passing ambulance siren from the street outside was suddenly so loud that Abe had to stop talking. When the sound tapered off, Abe resumed, talking off-script. "That siren reminded me of the day they took me to the hospital. I was conscious and aware, and I can still remember the siren sound very clearly to this day." He continued with the story.

"My condition got better after two weeks. I was then out of the coma. My wife told me that my three partners had taken turns staying at the hospital with me all that time, watching my every twitch and praying continuously for me." He stopped to take a deep breath. "When I was allowed visitors, our commuters visited me at the hospital. They all told me that the four of us, together with our employees, were like family to them. They said they were praying for me." He stopped to wipe his tears. Everyone was in tears. Then Teddy stood up to speak.

"While Abe was in a coma, the three of us decided to scrap the deal. We knew we could not handle the business without Abe's financial guidance. We told him our decision as soon as he was able to communicate with us. He said he was going to be okay. It was at this time that one of our commuters came to the hospital to talk to us."

"Frances—we called her Frankie—was a senior loan officer at a bank in New York City. She came to ask for the details and paperwork on the dealership and property deals. She said she might be able to help. She truly worked and negotiated with the persons involved in that deal." Teddy was now getting excited and speaking more hurriedly.

"She spoke to the owners of both properties, telling them that Abe had suffered a stroke and the deal might not go through. She was able to get the purchase price reduced even further. She also spoke to the two automakers. Their fear was that we, the original investors, were getting old and had no support management that could succeed us. At that time, my daughter, Maggie, was working for us as an accountant and studying for a bachelor's degree in business management at NYU. We promoted her and four other supervisors to manager-level jobs. The final loan was reduced by two million dollars." The audience felt good and applauded. Teddy continued.

"Still, we doubted ourselves. We were undecided." He paused. "It was Abe, from his hospital bed, who strongly encouraged us to go ahead with the deal." Teddy stopped for a moment; he was feeling emotional too.

Another siren was heard, but this time it was not as loud. Instead it sounded like it was coming from a few blocks away. Teddy continued. "In his slurred words, Abe advised us and reminded us that we had all come from the sewer and that we had dreamt of this very moment every day we were down there. He said that we are all growing old and will never get a chance for this kind of deal again. Abe was very confident of his decision. He was boldly unafraid of the future and was giving all the optimism that his numb and distressed body could muster." Teddy now looked at his three friends.

"The next day, all three of us went to the hospital with the loan contract. Billy signed it first as lead manager, and then all three of us signed it, including Abe. He signed it with his left and right hands." Teddy was about to end it when the applause started.

Everybody in the audience stood up to applaud. The applause was loud and prolonged. The siren grew louder and nearer. With the loud siren and the audience on their feet in enthusiastic applause, the four friends from the sewer were like the center of a parade in New York City's Canyon of Heroes, without the confetti. The four looked at the applauding audience and then looked at each other. They looked at how they appeared at that moment. Dressed sharply and handsomely, they knew they were far, far above the sewer system underneath the streets where their business dreams had started to take hold. Now, they were on top of the world.

SOLOMON, PETER, AND JOSEPH (A TRUE STORY)

This story will read like an investigator's names registry and travel assignment. There will be a lot of names mentioned along with the interesting places where they are. Most of them are involved in the search for solutions to a complex, ongoing challenge. I was one of so many who were touched by this subject in my early life, and then it became my constant concern. There were several stories that occurred at different periods that I linked together due to their common threads of exploitation and despair. This story aims to bring out some facts in the hope that they might help bring about a solution.

Our story starts here in Monmouth County, New Jersey.

Solomon Dwek was a resident of the affluent Deal Park neighborhood in Ocean Township. At thirty-six years old, Solomon was well respected and trusted due to the reputation of his parents, who founded a nonprofit Orthodox Jewish school, and to his appearance as a successful businessman. A real-estate investor and developer, Solomon was also the vice president of the school and was well known for his philanthropy inside and outside the Jewish community.[1]

In 2006, his reputation as a righteous, upstanding man suddenly came crashing down when it was revealed in the news that Solomon ran a real-estate empire based on a pyramid scheme under multiple business names. At that time, he owned 316 area properties. He was initially taken into custody by the FBI for a $50 million bank fraud.[2]

After his arrest, he agreed to become an undercover informant for the FBI in a widening sting operation called "Operation Bid Rig,"[3] which the feds had set up to gather evidence of corruption by local governments. Solomon was the perfect informant, or "stoolie" (stool pigeon), as they liked to call it. He looked honest and innocent and was very willing to do it for a reduced sentence for his crimes. It was in this undercover stint with the FBI that he met Peter.

Peter J. Cammarano III was the thirty-seventh mayor of the city of Hoboken, New Jersey. At age thirty-two, he was the youngest mayor the city had ever had. Hoboken, a city rich in tradition and history, was the setting of the first officially recorded baseball game in 1846, and it was the birthplace of singer/actor Frank Sinatra, its most famous son. In June 2009, the charismatic Peter Cammarano was in a very tight race for the mayoral election. He won the run-off election by a very slim margin of only 161 votes. As sweet as his hard-fought victory was, he did not stay on the job long enough to savor it. Just twenty-two days after assuming the office, Mayor Peter Cammarano was arrested in connection with Operation Bid Rig. He was charged with accepting twenty-five thousand dollars[4] in cash bribes in exchange for granting government contracts to an undercover cooperating witness named Solomon Dwek. Both Solomon and Peter had to admit their misconduct in the Newark federal courtroom of Joseph.

Jose L. Linares was the US District Court judge for the district of New Jersey. He was born in Havana, Cuba. He was twelve years old in 1965 when his family escaped Fidel Castro's revolution takeover of Cuba. He graduated from the Temple University Beasley School of Law in Philadelphia. He was a judge on the Essex County Superior Court in 2002 when he was nominated by President George W. Bush to a seat on the US District Court in New Jersey.[5] He presided over the cases of Solomon Dwek and Peter Cammarano.

Recalling his childhood experiences in Cuba and his upbringing in the tough neighborhoods of Newark, New Jersey, Judge Linares told Bob Braun of the *Star-Ledger,* "You can't have experiences like those I did and not have a sense of the injustice inherent in total government control."[6] He sentenced Solomon Dwek to six years in prison and Peter Cammarano to two years.

The Feds' Operation Bid Rig turned out to be a bigger, wider net of elaborate and simultaneous sting operations that targeted not just corrupt politicians but also international money launderers. Sixty politicians and politically connected individuals were indicted as a result of this sweeping FBI sting. It was like an open clothesline that exposed all the filthy underwear worn beneath the flashy politicians' suits. For me, it also uncovered a subject I am always readily attuned to—the illegal kidney trade.

My first wife, Raquel, passed away due to lupus nephritis in Manila in 1980, when we were both twenty-nine years old. Her illness started with a mild urinary tract infection, something she was managing quite well. It wasn't long, however, until she took a turn for the worse and had to start going through dialysis treatments. Dialysis is a medical treatment that uses a machine to remove waste and excess water from the blood as an artificial replacement for kidney function. Losing a beloved spouse at that young age left me with a very dark, rudderless outlook on life. So every time I hear the word *kidney*, it gets my attention.

The wide reach of Operation Bid Rig also uncovered, to my shock and amazement, an illegal trafficker of kidneys. His name is Levy Izhak Rosenbaum,[7] he is a resident of Brooklyn, New York. On July 29, 2009, *The New York Times* reported the arrest of Rosenbaum, who had openly admitted that for ten years he had illegally brokered the sale of kidneys. In fact, at the time of his arrest, he was in the middle of negotiating the sale of a kidney to a wealthy transplant patient for $160,000. He revealed that the kidney donor was a young, healthy, and obviously needy man from Israel who was given a measly $10,000. That was when I became aware that the illegal trafficking of kidneys was, and remains, a very profitable trade.

Four years after Operation Bid Rig, in May 2013, I was flipping through the television channels when I saw a documentary on HBO that featured people who looked like me, in settings familiar to me, and speaking my language. It was titled *Tales from the Organ Trade*.[8] A long segment of the eighty-two-minute documentary was filmed in impoverished neighborhoods of the city of Manila and Quezon Province in the Philippines. I saw Filipino men, aged twenty-five to forty-five, willingly lift their shirts up to expose the scars on the left and right sides of their abdomens. The scars were from kidney-extraction surgeries. From the squalid, overcrowded slums of Manila, we heard the life struggles of Jo-Boy and Eddie-Boy.[9]

Jo-Boy was a forty-four-year-old unemployed resident of the slums. If there were sublevels of a slum caste, he would probably be at the lowest level. He lived with his family in the bottom half of a makeshift house, where he could not even stand up. He had to sit on the door floor first and then crawl on his hands and knees to get into the windowless dwelling he called home. That's how poor he was. He was approached about donating one of his kidneys by a street-smart lady named Diane, an organ-donation "broker" in the slums who had also donated one of her kidneys for a price. The agreed-upon price for Jo-Boy's kidney was $2,500, a large amount of money for a poor person in a country in which the current exchange rate is about forty pesos to a dollar. It was to be a once-in-a-lifetime cash bonanza for a long-time slum dweller like Jo-Boy. The intended recipient of Jo-Boy's kidney was a wealthy lady who lived in one of the affluent suburbs of Manila. But before the operation was to get underway, Diane and Jo-Boy had to be clear with the law.

The Philippines is one of many countries in which exchanging kidneys for cash remains illegal. The donation must always have an altruistic intent, or the operation will not be approved by hospital management. So for that dreaded hospital pre-operation interview, Diane had to patiently and carefully coach Jo-Boy on his kidney donation story. Jo-Boy was to inform the hospital that his mother had worked for this rich kidney-recipient lady for a long time, and now that his mother is dead and the rich lady needs a kidney transplant, he was willing to donate one of his kidneys to her as a token of gratitude, without any monetary compensation."[10]

Teary-eyed, Jo-Boy admitted on camera that he felt conflicted about his kidney donation. He said, "I know what I'm about to do is against the laws of God and the laws of man, but I am willing to make the sacrifice to get out of this life of poverty!" Sadly, his operation did not proceed as he had hoped. The lady recipient asked for a younger donor, so he was rejected and twenty-two-year old Eddie-Boy was tapped instead. Eddie-Boy was also a resident of the slums in which Jo-Boy lived. Eddie-Boy stated on-camera that when he got his kidney-donation payment, he would go back to his home province and start a chicken and pig farm. That did not happen either. Another slum dweller, Hector, ended up donating his kidney and getting the cash.[11] I mentioned these personal stories to show that there are so many willing to be paid donors, mostly in poor countries like the Philippines, India, Pakistan, China, and Bangladesh.

A nephrology surgeon from Turkey (we'll call him Dr. T)[12] and another from Israel (we'll call him

Dr. I)[13] do not believe that their kidney surgeries, clandestine as they may be, are wrong. They believe firmly that they are saving lives. Both have done surgeries mainly in Kosovo's capital of Pristina, where their clinic used to be until it was closed down by Kosovo police.

"I am saving people's lives. People want to live, and no one can change that,"[14] Dr. I said on-camera. Both doctors also believed that the kidney-transplant medical procedure must be allowed legally, with safeguards and regulations.

To understand this massive organ-donation problem, let's get to know the basics of this organ and its functions. Every person has two kidneys. Our kidneys are the bean-shaped organs about the size of our fists that are located near the middle of our back, just below the rib cage. Our kidneys work like sophisticated trash collectors. Every day, our kidneys process about two hundred quarts of blood in order to sift out about two quarts of waste product and extra water. The waste and extra water later become urine.[16]

The waste in our blood comes from the normal breakdown of active muscle and from the food we eat. Our body uses the food for energy and self-repair. After our body has taken what it needs from the food, the leftover waste is sent to the blood. When our kidneys fail to remove these wastes, they build up in the blood and damage our body. Our kidneys also have the task of maintaining a healthy balance of fluids and electrolytes (salt compounds).[17] Nephrology is the branch of medical study that covers the kidneys.

As with our paired limbs (we have two feet, two hands, and two eyes), we also have two kidneys. The fact that we have two kidneys adds to the mystique of and interest in this subject. That is, people say that there must be a reason why we have two kidneys, considering that it has been determined that our body can function fairly well with only one. A good example is eighty-five-year-old former Philippines president Fidel V. Ramos.[18] Despite having only one kidney, he had a great military and political career, having led the revolution against the Marcos dictatorship. Publicly, he admits to having only one kidney but does not reveal the reason why that is. He remains active at his age and continues to live a full, healthy life.

In 1954, surgeons performed the first-ever successful kidney transplant between identical twins at Boston's Brigham and Women's Hospital.[19] Since then, kidney transplants have become accepted medical practice for end-stage organ failure, saving or extending the lives of thousands of people. Due to the lack of international regulations, kidney brokers, or middlemen, have come out to match prospective kidney recipients with donors from poor countries. These brokers charge patients an exorbitant amount of money and pay a very small amount to the poor, illiterate donors. For these middlemen, the illegal lure of "transplant tourism" will remain a very profitable trade. They strongly claim that they are saving lives, but what they don't admit is the enormous amount of money they make from every kidney transplant.

What does the Catholic Church say about kidney donation? Father Joseph Son Nguyen, the lead chaplain at UC Irvine Medical Center, said on May 31, 2015 that "in the image of God the Creator, Christians are called to live an authentic culture of life, which is built up by gestures of sharing. Organ donation is encouraged because it is an edifying example of living out the gospel of life."[20] Father Joseph points to Pope John Paul II as his guide. In his position on the subject, the Pontiff wrote, "A particularly praiseworthy example of such gestures is the donation of organs, performed in an <u>ethically acceptable manner</u>, with a view to offering a chance of health and even life itself to the sick who sometimes have no other hope" (*Evangelium Vitae*, no. 86).[21]

I underlined the words "ethically acceptable manner" because these three words define why kidney-donation regulatory laws have not come about in most countries today. In the underground kidney trade, both donors and recipients are financially exploited. Surprisingly, the only country in the world that has lawfully and successfully regulated the donation of organs is Iran.

In the Islamic Republic of Iran, people wait to donate a kidney, not the other way around. "With its extensive censorship, women's rights and security issues, Iran's liberal stance on other controversial matters is thought provoking,"[22] wrote Allison Kushner from the Foreign Policy Association. People who need kidneys get them rapidly rather than die on the waiting list. "Every year, approximately 1,400 Iranians sell one of their kidneys to someone they do not know."[23] With good design and regulation, Iran has developed a system that pays for donors so the system does not need to be exploitive or immoral. In Iran, the legal kidney market has prevented the development of the abusive black markets and kidney tourism seen in other countries. As the kidney-shortage crisis intensifies, governments should look closely at what Iran has achieved.

Iran began paying kidney donors out of necessity. Their revolution of 1979, when they overthrew the ruling shah, proved to be a very difficult financial period for the country. The United States led the confiscation of Iran's assets abroad, and its treasury was further drained by the eight-year Iran-Iraq war. There was little money for dialysis and no physical or legal infrastructure for getting kidneys from deceased donors. So Iran began allowing donors to be paid, first in a private system and then, in the mid-1990s, in a state-regulated system in which the government paid donors the equivalent of about $3,500 in Iranian currency, labeling the sum a gift for their altruism. By 1999, their waiting list for kidneys was essentially eliminated. Today, due to successful government regulation together with charitable donations, the government-set price for a donated kidney is between about $2,000 and $4,000.[24] It is also a system that provides continuous medical care for both donor and recipient after the transplant surgery.

Think about this: Nobel Laureate economists Gary Becker and Julio Elias have estimated that a payment of $15,000 for living donors would alleviate the shortage of kidneys in the United States. They wrote that whoever pays this donation compensation, whether government or insurance companies, will save money in the long run since transplant is cheaper than prolonged dialysis treatments.[25] In the same report in 2010 on the Health Policy Blog, it was written that Singapore was preparing to pay its donors $36,000 for their donated organs.[26]

In 2006, Dr. Arthur Matas of the University of Minnesota wrote a paper for the American Society of Nephrology titled "Why We Should Develop a Regulated System of Kidney Sales: A Call to Action!"[27] Without citing the successful Iranian system, he wrote about the advantages of a similar regulated system here in the United States, adding that the system should "treat the kidney donor with dignity and appreciation for providing a lifesaving gift."

In May 2008, the World Health Organization condemned organ commercialism, which, as I wrote earlier, targets the vulnerable populations of poor countries. It was in Istanbul, Turkey, that the WHO urged their fellow transplant professionals, individually and through their organizations, to conclude that kidney commercialism should be prohibited. It was called the "Istanbul Declaration." They all agreed to "put an end to these unethical activities and foster safe, accountable practices that meet the needs of transplant recipients while protecting donors." It further stated that "this declaration should reinforce the resolve of governments and international organizations to develop laws and guidelines to bring an end to wrongful practices…and preserve the nobility of organ donation."[28]

According to the National Kidney Foundation, as of January 11, 2016, the number of people waiting for kidneys in the United States was 100,791, a critically high number. Thirteen people die each day while waiting for a life-saving kidney transplant. Every fourteen minutes someone is added to the kidney-transplant waiting list.[29] The National Living Donor Assistance Center (NLDAC) provides financial assistance to those who want to donate an organ to cover the donor's (and a companion) travel and lodging expenses.[30] I watched their very informative video, which I believe covers all aspects of living donation. But there was no mention of a financial

incentive for the unrelated, non-altruistic living donor, and I believe this type of donor could increase
the available kidneys for transplantation, as they did
in Iran.

Kidney patients who have no altruistic donors
will be gathering their savings and possibly borrow-
ing money from sympathetic relatives and friends to
have transplants done abroad. "Transplant tourism,"
as they call it, is the harvesting of live kidneys from
poor, usually illiterate donors. I don't blame them
for seeking life-saving transplant surgeries despite
the high risks and high costs. It costs so much more
to keep patients in life-prolonging dialysis treatments than it does to have them undergo life-saving
organ transplants. In the meantime, those unscru-
pulous organ middlemen will be raking in a lot of
money, justifying their greed by saying that they are
saving lives. There is no doubt that they are.

On April 9, 2012, the Food and Drug Administration
reported that they are monitoring three products for
patients with end-stage renal disease (ESRD) for potential participation in the FDA's Innovation Pathway,
an evolving system designed to help medical devices
reach patients in a safe, timely, and collaborative manner. These three products are:[31]

1. An implantable Renal Assist Device (iRAD)
    being developed by the University of California,
    San Francisco.

2. A Wearable Artificial Kidney (WAK) in development by Blood Purification Technologies Inc. of Beverly Hills, California.
3. A Hemoaccess Valve System (HVS) that has been designed by CreatiVasc Medical, based in Greenville, South Carolina.

The FDA report did not specify when these devices may be available to patients. A friend of mine who is currently undergoing dialysis treatments and is patiently waiting for these devices heard that one of them may be available in 2017. That's great. Let's hope that they work the way they were meant to and allow patients to live longer. They have suffered enough.

You have now read the statements of kidney patients, kidney donors, the Catholic Church, Nobel Laureates in economics, and practicing nephrologists who recommend a compensated and regulated kidney-donation system. You have also read alarming statistics from the National Kidney Foundation. The most burning question is, why can't we start a compensated and regulated kidney-donation system here in the United States patterned after that of Iran? I don't know. There must be some reasons keeping the agencies we rely on, such as the US Health Department, the American Society of Nephrology, and the National Kidney Foundation, from working together and forming such an urgent regulatory donation body. Maybe, just maybe, a small group of compassionate nephrology practitioners, working with lawmakers, can start the path to this kidney-donation system that could grow into a nationwide nonprofit agency. Please remember that thirteen people die every day while on the transplant waiting list.

You might be wondering why I titled this story using the biblical names of Solomon, Peter and Joseph. It was when I read about Operation Bid Rig that I saw the name of the first illegal-kidney middleman identified in the news. These middlemen normally work in the shadows of the organ black market. We cannot allow them to go on. I also hope that by bringing this subject to the surface, we might find a Joseph, someone who can stop the scourge of callous middlemen and, someday soon, pave the way for the kidney-donation system we so urgently need.

Update: On July 19, 2016, I saw a Facebook story about a new artificial kidney developed by researchers at the University of California, San Francisco. If you go back to my story above, this is the first artificial kidney that the FDA is helping to develop. It is still a square block, and the size is bigger than a fist, making it too big to implant into a human patient. UCSF is working to make it smaller. This could be the best alternative to human kidney transplants.

<u>References</u>:

1. "Solomon Dwek," Wikipedia, April, 2016.
2. "Solomon Dwek," Wikipedia, April, 2016.
3. "Solomon Dwek," Wikipedia, April, 2016.
4. "Peter Cammarano," Wikipedia, April, 2016.
5. Braun, Bob, Star-Ledger columnist, February 7, 2010.
6. Braun, Bob, Star-Ledger columnist.
7. Tao, Dominic, The New York Times, July 29, 2009.
8. "Tales from the Organ Trade, documentary film by Ric Esther Beinstock, an Associated Producers Ltd. Production (winner of two Amnesty International Awards, four Canadian Screen Awards, the Edward R. Murrow Award, and the Jack R. Howard Award).
9. Tales from the Organ Trade," documentary film.
10. "Tales from the Organ Trade," documentary film.
11. "Tales from the Organ Trade," documentary film.
12. "Tales from the Organ Trade," documentary film.
13. "Tales from the Organ Trade," documentary film.
14. "Tales from the Organ Trade," documentary film.

16. "Your Kidneys and How They Work," WebMD, June 25, 2016

17. "Your Kidneys and How They Work," WebMD, June 25, 2016

18. "Fidel V. Ramos Does 31 Push-ups," You Tube film, Oct. 15, 2015

19. "Kidney Transplant Program," Brigham and Women's Hospital website, April 26, 2016

20. Jones, Jenna, "What are the Church's Guidelines on Organ Donation," Orange County Catholic website (Diocese of Orange County, California, USA), May 31, 2015.

21. Jones, Jenna, "What are the Church Guidelines on Organ Donation," . . .

22. Kushner, Allison, "Selling Organs in Iran," Foreign Policy Association, Foreign Policy Blogs.

23. Kushner, Allison, "Selling Organs in Iran," . . .

24. Kushner, Allison, "Selling Organs in Iran," . . .

25. Goodman, John, "What We Can Learn from Iran about Organ Donation," Health Policy Blog, NCPA.org

26. Goodman, John, "What We Can Learn from Iran about Organ Donation," . . .

27. Matas, Arthur, J., "Why We Should Develop a Regulated System of Kidney Sales: A Call to Action!" Clinical Journal of the American Society of Nephrology, October, 2006.

28. "The Declaration of Istanbul on Organ Trafficking and Transplant Tourism," Clinical Journal of the American Society of Nephrology, August, 2008.
29. "Organ Donation and Transplantation Statistics," National Kidney Foundation, data gathered on July 4, 2016.
30. National Living Donor Assistance Center (NLDAC), National Kidney Foundation, data gathered July 4, 2016.
31. Jefferson, Erica, US FDA Press Announcements, April 9, 2012.

KABOOM!

The final decision to take one's own life could also be a comforting and de-stressing turn. Relief from the relentless pressures that led to that decision may give one the calm and clarity of mind to think of the best method to carry out this ultimate act. The goal is to quickly cross over into a state in which the arduous burdens of living are no longer present. That could be so tempting to a person who has constantly tried and failed to face the challenges we humans go through every day. Some of you reading this may at one time or another have contemplated, or are currently contemplating, this dark subject. I hope this story prompts a timely and decisive change of heart.

Two forty-five in the afternoon was when employees at BrashBurger planned to bring out the surprise birthday cake for Joe that Thursday. Everyone on the dinner crew, which starts at three o'clock, had been notified of Joe's surprise birthday cake and been asked to come early for it. But no one from that shift even came on time. Joe's colleagues from the morning shift sang the birthday song for him and brought out the small, round chocolate cake with the two lit candles, numbers 2 and 3 that they'd bought from the grocery store next door. Joe blew out the candles as prompted. He smiled at them, thanked them for their efforts, and offered to slice the cake for them. They all thanked Joe and told him to take the whole cake home. One of the girls put it back into the box and gave it to Joe on his way out.

It was raining that afternoon as Joe, carrying the plastic bag with his untouched birthday cake, waited for the bus at the covered stop. He wiped the tears from his eyes as he saw the approaching bus slow down. He rode the bus to his stop, got off on his street, and took his time as he walked four blocks in the heavy rain to his small rented room. Drenched as he turned his door key, he placed the cake on the table. With his clothes dripping wet, he sat down in his lone dining chair and wept. He just wanted to die.

To Joe, it seemed like nothing ever worked out well for him. His mother, believed to be a teenager when she gave birth to him, had left him wrapped in a warm winter coat at a fire station when he was an infant. She had disappeared with another man and was never heard from again. There was very little information on his real father. Some said he was in jail, others said he went back to the South and was probably dead. He had not heard from his biological father in all these years, so he did not make the effort to look for him, either. He just shrugged his shoulders at those curious questions. No grandparents were there during his childhood, just the foster-care system. He'd drifted from one foster home to another, unable to stay long enough to feel the warmth of a loving family.

School was a struggle for Joe. He did not have the concentration for numbers or letters in kindergarten. It was a very patient kindergarten teacher named Ms. Ferguson who had spent time teaching him to read and write so he would not fall behind the other kids. She was the first role model for Joe. Aside from her patience, she was also pleasant and nurturing, especially toward Joe, whose home life, she knew, was burdened with despair and dysfunction. On her own time, she tutored Joe during school lunch breaks, and Joe responded to her effort with an eagerness to learn. But she'd left the school when Joe was in the middle of third grade, and Joe did not know why. By then, Joe knew enough reading and writing to get by in school.

It was in high school, when Joe started classes in algebra, geometry, chemistry, and trigonometry that he once again fell behind. For a while, he stayed with a foster family in whose house he shared a bedroom with a kind and smart older foster brother, Brando. Brando taught him these subjects as patiently as Ms. Ferguson had. But when Joe was starting his junior year in high school, Brando's family had to move to Canada for his father's work assignment. Circumstances did not allow for Joe to go with them. Joe moved to another foster home, where he stayed until he was eighteen. On his eighteenth birthday, Joe was on his own.

Joe had known he was not the brightest kid in his school. On a scale from one to ten, he would be a four, not even half smart. College or trade school would only be a waste of time. Instead, with the good work ethic that he knew he had, he worked several jobs, sometimes two or three at a time.

He would deliver newspapers during early mornings, wrapping the papers in plastic at the news depot in Eatontown, New Jersey, starting at four o'clock and delivering them in his beat-up car until seven o'clock. Despite the gas cost and car maintenance, the pay was decent. Right after that, he'd go straight to BrashBurger and clock in for the busy morning shift. At three o'clock, he'd go home and sleep until eight thirty. Then he'd go to work at the food store next to BrashBurger, stocking shelves from nine o'clock until midnight. It was exhausting. It was also unsafe.

It was in the early hours of Thanksgiving morning, during the cold, early snow, that Joe's car had skidded uncontrollably into an oncoming car as he made a turn. It was his news-depot boss, Fritz, whose face he'd first seen when he opened his eyes at the hospital.

"You had a car accident, Joe!"

"How did it happen? I am a very careful driver!" He could not believe he'd had an accident.

"The other driver was a college student who had been driving for four hours trying to get home for Thanksgiving." Fritz had had to pause for a moment. "I think you were both sleep deprived."

"How is the other guy? Is he okay?"

"He's alive. He's in worse shape than you are, but the doctors said he will be okay."

Joe had lost his driver's license because of the accident. He could no longer deliver newspapers or work the late-night shift at the food store. BrashBurger valued his hard work and dedication and kept him an employee. He lost a large amount of income. His life, the seemingly unlucky, ungifted, aimless, friendless life that he'd had during his twenty-three years, was all that he thought of as he walked in the rain for four blocks on his birthday.

He sat still in his wet clothes for about two hours. He then took off the wet clothes and went to bed without having dinner. There was one thing he had decided to do with his life that he had been contemplating for the last few months. He just wanted to die. He wanted to end it all. He was alone, and he had very little money. His future, as far as he could see, was just the BrashBurger job. As he had been doing lately, he kept trying to think of any reason to go on living. There was none. His mind was made up.

His alarm clock sounded at five thirty the next morning, as usual. It was his day off. Today was the day, he decided. He was going to find a way to kill himself. A painless, quick, and sure way to die.

Planning a suicide, after one has made the decision to carry it out, is a great relief. Like a depressured valve, all of his life's pressures were now removed from Joe's mind, and another new subject had fully taken over. Joe felt good. He took a shower and fixed himself a breakfast of coffee, toast, and jelly. Then he got out and decided to walk on the busy main street. As he took a leisurely stroll, a number of ideas for how to commit suicide, some of which he'd researched, were all bouncing around in his mind.

Taking rat poison was a sure way to die, but it would burn the lining of his stomach and might take longer than he wanted. He was also worried at the permanent damage it would do to his body if it failed to work. Nope, he would not want to live with the disability.

He could jump off the George Washington Bridge. He'd heard of some doing it successfully. But he'd also heard that some of those who had attempted it were unsuccessful. They did not die. The sudden impact of one's body on the water could instead leave a person with severe neck injuries. Nope, the results were not guaranteed.

Some were creative enough to use just their leather belts to hang themselves. This could be simple enough for him. Hanging from his belt could be a good option.

He stopped at the intersection. As he lifted his head to look up to the traffic light, something colorful caught his eye from about one block away. He walked closer to find out what it was. It was a red, white, and blue US Army recruitment poster, with the smiling picture of a recruitment officer on it. His attention was drawn to the officer's name, Sergeant Reginald Flowers.

There was a confident smile on the face of Sergeant Flowers. His clean-shaven jaw was tight, his graying, thinly cut sideburns showed manly maturity, and his eyes showed pleasant friendliness. Joe felt he wanted to see him. Joe opened the glass door and saw the officer look up from the paperwork he was reading.

"Come in, son," he said and stood up, ready for a handshake. Joe could not resist shaking his hand. "I'm Sergeant Flowers. And what is your name, son?"

"My name is Joe." To Joe, Sergeant Flowers, with his graying hair, looked older than his poster picture.

"Please sit down, Joe."

They both sat down and talked. Curiosity had now replaced the despair in Joe's uncertain mind. He looked at the officer's crisp, well-fitting khaki uniform and the multicolored buttons on his left chest. Sergeant Flowers's arms were refined yet muscular. They were not the rugged arms of a combat soldier that Joe was expecting. The sergeant moved smartly, even gracefully, as he walked toward the steel filing cabinet to hand Joe the forms he had to complete. Joe was impressed.

"I will call you next week to schedule you for a full physical exam. Once you pass that physical, you will report for basic training at Fort Benning in Columbus, Georgia," the sergeant told him.

Joe was excited. His gruesome suicide thoughts after the years of continuous despair had been placed on hold. He now looked forward to doing military stuff, like boarding a plane to Georgia and wearing that crisp US Army uniform. The army, as per his new vision, would be his new family. He passed all the tests and was enlisted.

Afghanistan was the hotbed war theatre that Joe volunteered for. He was the first one to sign up. His earlier suicidal thoughts had made him totally fearless, brave, and questfully daring. He never told anyone in his army family that not too long ago he had seriously considered the idea of suicide. Now he was serving and fighting for his country, a more honorable calling than dipping raw, cut potatoes into boiling oil at BrashBurger.

Joe became the model soldier. He would volunteer to lead reconnaissance missions and would be the front man in the pack, right after the minesweeping unit cleared the area. For all the unfortunate events that had happened in his life, he found he had a special, God-given gift—a sharp eye. He could shoot the enemy with sharp precision, thus avoiding dreaded friendly fire. He was shot and wounded while saving the lives of some platoon brothers by affording them cover. All of these things he did with pride and enthusiasm. For all his bravery and valor, he was awarded the Distinguished Service Cross.

It was the day of the medal-awarding ceremony in Afghanistan. The sun was shining brightly, the army marching band was playing a John Philip Sousa tune, and the American flag and regiment flags were unfurled for a parade. The defense secretary, who had flown in for the occasion, pinned the medal on the left side of Joe's chest, thanking him for his "unparalleled heroism." His whole regiment and two other three-star generals cheered as the secretary shook his hand. Joe's face was filled with pride and honor. "Being alive is great," he thought. "I don't want to die anymore. I don't even want to think of taking my life anymore." He could not help but tear up as he recalled his years of despair. Every life is precious, he realized, most especially his own.

It was at the reception following the medal-ceremony that he met a pretty Afghan girl named Aliah. Her hijab covered her head and chest but revealed a shy, pretty face. She was even prettier, Joe had observed, at the rare moments when she smiled.

"Congratulations, sir." She spoke softly to Joe when they were introduced.

"Thank you, Aliah. I'm glad you came here today!" Joe learned that Aliah was a grade-school teacher and the niece of one of the top-ranked Afghan military officers. She spoke enough English to carry on a pleasant, interesting conversation with Joe.

"I heard you were very brave; thank you for saving the lives of our Afghan soldiers," she said. They were the best words of gratitude Joe had ever heard, better than the carefully worded praises of the defense secretary. Joe was immediately smitten, and he did not want this sweet moment to end. He just wanted to be with Aliah. He tried to impress her.

"Do you want to hold my medal, Aliah?" Without a response from her, Joe unpinned the medal from his chest and handed it to her.

"I hope I do not drop it!" She smiled as she accepted the brass medal and ribbon from Joe, who was a very proud man at that moment. Hers was the sweetest face, and she had the sweetest smile he had ever seen in his life. Right away, he fell in love with her.

The song "A Certain Smile," sung by Johnny Mathis, echoed romantically from the jukebox at the barracks mess hall that evening. "Our hero is in love!" Joe's army buddies teased him. That night, Joe relived his whole sad life again up to this day. He remembered the loneliness, the failures, and how, at each juncture, someone or something always prevented him from killing himself. He recalled his teacher, Ms. Ferguson, who had had the kindest words and unequalled perseverance to teach him. There was also his stepbrother and best friend, Brando, who had taught him most of what he knew today. Then he thought of his mother. She would have been proud of him, he thought. He would have dedicated his medal to her, if only she were here. If only he knew her.

Afghan traditions allow Muslim men to marry non-Muslim women, but a Muslim woman cannot marry a non-Muslim man. It was a heartbreaking tradition for Joe, since Aliah was a traditional Muslim. Asking her for a date was just impossible. For a woman to be seen in public with a non-Muslim man was a crime. So how could they meet again?

We should never underestimate the cleverness and persistence of a man in love. Joe told his commanding officer that he wanted to lead a patrol in the town where Aliah's school was. It was a routine peacekeeping and public-relations patrol in which army soldiers get to meet the community members and interact with the locals to prove to them that they are friendly protectors. One morning, Joe was able to pass a note to Aliah. During the next morning's patrol, Aliah passed a note in reply to Joe. She wrote that she wanted to meet Joe at a cavern on the rocky northern hill that bordered the next town. Joe knew that place was isolated and safe to meet.

Joe was ecstatic. All his suicide thoughts were now totally extinguished. For the first time in his young life, he could dream. It was like waking up to a new reality. Everything around him looked bright and positive; not even the word *impossible* could deter his resolve. And, no matter how impossible marriage might be in this forbidding, complex country, becoming Aliah's husband would be a relished, joyful dream that he wanted to come true.

Before his much-anticipated rendezvous with Aliah, Joe, together with two of his army buddies, went to a jewelry store downtown to get an engagement ring. Downtown was a safe area patrolled diligently by local police. He picked out a silver ring with a decent-sized stone—not too big, not too small. It took him two hours to decide on the best-looking ring for his sweet love. It had to be the perfect ring.

Joe arrived at the cavern early, but he found that Aliah had gotten there even earlier and was waiting for him. From a few yards away, Joe saw that she was sitting on a knee-high rock. She looked like a black dot under the bright midday sun. She was wearing a full-length, black burka that covered her whole body. Only her eyes could be seen through a netted cloth that was part of her garb. Joe noticed her sad yet unusually defiant face, but his excitement over this secret meeting was overwhelming, and he failed to notice anything else.

"I love you, Aliah! You might be sad because you think that we cannot fall in love, but we can. As long as we love each other, we can overcome anything." Joe tried to assure her.

"It is impossible. You and I are not meant to love!" Her response was forceful, unlike the soft, shy tone she had had at their first meeting.

Joe took out the small blue-velvet ring box from his pocket and opened it to show her. "This ring will prove my love for you, Aliah. You are the first woman who made me fall in love." Joe was now on his knees. "I will love you forever, Aliah, for as long as you wear this ring on your finger."

"I can see your sincerity, Joe, but I cannot accept that." She looked at the ring but did not extend her hand to accept it. Joe insisted on giving her the ring despite the rejection, and he tried to explain.

"Let me tell you something, Aliah. Before I met you, my life was miserable and hopeless. I was despairing, and I wanted to kill myself. But now that I have you, I feel so full of hope and love, and I want to live as long as I can be with you! You have changed the way I view life, Aliah, and I want to spend the rest of my life with you!" Joe was in tears as he tried hard to voice his emotions about how he had been transformed by love. Again he offered the ring to her, and again she looked at it but did not accept it.

"It's a beautiful ring, Joe. It must have been expensive!" Aliah said, unmoved by the beautifully crafted piece of jewelry. Joe took the ring gently from the blue-velvet box and asked for her hand, but she kept her hand under her burka, unwilling to be touched. Joe could not believe that this tender moment, a moment he had long dreamed of, was slipping away.

"Why, Aliah? What is wrong?" Joe could not believe it.

"Let me tell you something also, Joe!" This time, her face turned vengeful. "I cannot marry someone like you who continue to kill my people! How many of my people have you killed, Joe? Fifty, maybe a hundred?" Her voice turned louder as she pointed her finger accusingly at Joe. "The men you are killing are my cousins and uncles and friends!" She looked at Joe with much anger. Joe was not ready for this sudden hostile sentiment.

"But we came here to give you a better life, to remove those who have ruled you in terror! Your uncle is a military officer and is fighting with us. Can't you see why we are doing this?" he said.

Aliah stood up with her hands and voice raised. "My uncle is a traitor to our country. He too has killed many of his own people. That dog will pay for his choices. He will be beheaded, and his body will be dragged in the streets and left in the desert for the vultures to feast on!"

Joe had to step back in disbelief. He couldn't believe that his dreamy, tender moment had become filled with fiery, revolutionary rhetoric. "Aliah, why are you so angry at me? I came here to give you this ring as a symbol of my love for you. You are the only woman I have ever loved in my life. Please, let us talk about this!" He tried to tone down her angry outburst, but she wouldn't let him. She grabbed the ring box from Joe's hand and threw it away. It landed on the rocks. Joe watched the box slip and disappear into the deep rock crevices. He tried to get closer to Aliah to touch her and calm her down. Beneath the netted cloth of her burka, Joe could see her face. That sweet, innocent face that he had fallen in love with had become a fiery picture of hate. Hate for him and the uniform he wore and the shining medal still firmly pinned on his chest.

"Do you know what I have underneath this burka, Joe?" This time, she started walking toward Joe, who had to step back. "I have a belt strapped with bombs and enough shrapnel to kill both of us. Joe, this is my gift to you to thank you for your stupid ring!" She pulled out a string, which Joe believed was the bomb detonator.

With the agility of a trained soldier, Joe lunged at Aliah to stop her from detonating her shrapnel-filled body bomb. He pleaded with her, "No, Aliah, no!" But his plea was in vain. He was too late.

Kaboom!

It was silent for a moment after the loud explosion. Thick smoke enveloped the cavern where they were. Joe looked around and saw blood everywhere. He felt that he was floating as he was lifted up from the bombed cavern. He looked down, searching for Aliah. All he could see was her black, tattered burka draped on one of the knee-high rocks close to where she had previously sat. Joe was drifting higher and farther away from the burka. "I must be dead," he thought. It was getting darker as the moments passed, and he continued to float upward and away.

Joe felt himself land on his feet inside a dark place. There was a pale, distant light coming from the east. From that faint light, he sensed that he was walking inside a tunnel, moving toward the direction of the light. He walked about thirteen steps and then saw the figure of another person walking toward the light. It was the back side of a woman with long, brown hair. She looked very familiar to Joe.

"Ms. Ferguson?" He yelled her name, and the woman turned around slowly.

"Yes, it's me, Joe!" She smiled as they walked together at the same slow pace.

"You left the school when I was in third grade. Why?" Joe asked her. She was smiling as she remembered Joe's early school years.

"Yes, Joe, and I'm so sorry that I did not say good-bye to you. You were one of those students who showed a lot of promise. But you needed guidance, which I was glad to have given you."

"I learned that you moved to another school. Why?" Joe asked, truly curious about her decision.

"I married my college sweetheart and moved to a nearby state. I taught grade school there too, and I met more students like you. I tutored them also. Teaching fulfilled me. It was my life's work."

Joe had to ask the dreaded question. "Are you dead too?"

"Yes, Joe. I am not alive anymore."

"How did you die, Ms. Ferguson?"

"There was a man who entered our school one morning with a fully loaded gun and started shooting. One of his bullets killed me." Joe was saddened that a shooting had taken the life of his favorite teacher and mentor. He went on seeking answers from Ms. Ferguson until they came to a slight bend to the right in the dark tunnel. Ms. Ferguson stopped walking and faced her former student.

"It was nice meeting you again, Joe, but this is where I stop. You have to keep walking toward the light at the end of the tunnel." She paused, smiled proudly, and told him, "I saw that you got the army medal. I knew you would get it someday." She paused again and then added, "And by the way, Joe, do you remember that day when you decided you wanted to kill yourself?"

"How did you know that?"

"I was there with you, Joe. I was the one who guided you to walk down Main Street toward the army recruitment office." She smiled as she told him about her last good deed for him.

"Thank you very much, Ms. Ferguson!"

"I was glad you felt my prayers and walked that way."

Joe was filled with gratitude. "Thank you for continuing to guide me."

"Good-bye, Joe!" She stepped to the left, walking farther from Joe and disappeared into the darkness.

Joe walked another few steps and saw another image walking in front of him in the dark. He recognized this one too.

"Brando?"

"Yes, Joe, it's me, your foster brother and best friend!" They hugged each other, or at least they felt like they did.

"Are you dead too, Brando?"

"Yes, Joe, I died of a drug overdose when I was in college."

"But you always avoided drugs, even cigarettes."

"College was when I experimented with drugs. I had so much free time on campus. When we were in high school, I spent most of my time tutoring you in your science subjects. That kept me out of trouble. I was lonely in college, and I got involved with the wrong crowd."

"I thought you would have been a successful engineer by now, like you had planned."

"That was my life goal, but goals are moving targets. Sometimes you get there, sometimes you don't."

"You would have been a great engineer, Brando. You're very smart. Think of the many things you would have built."

"Well, you got the army cross medal, and that was what I had wished for you, my brother. And I'm happy you got it. Your medal was an achievement for me too." They came to a left bend in the tunnel, and Brando stopped walking.

"This is as far as I go, Joe. You have to keep walking to reach the end of the tunnel." Brando paused. They hugged again, and then Brando had some parting words. "By the way, Joe, do you remember when you decided you wanted to kill yourself and you were walking on Main Street?"

"Yes, I remember."

"I was the one who guided you to look up so you would see that army recruitment poster." Brando smiled.

"Thank you very much, Brando. Thank you for continuing to guide me."

"Even in death, Joe, we continue to care for those we love." He paused and then said, "Good-bye, Joe!" Brando stepped to the right and slowly disappeared.

Joe kept walking toward the light, which was now shining much brighter. He knew he was getting near it. He kept thinking of Ms. Ferguson and Brando, the two people who had given their time and their love to him, even after life. They were very well-intentioned human beings but their lives were unexpectedly cut short. Joe started thinking.

Was my death untimely too? Joe asked himself. If he had killed himself like he had planned to do, would he be trying to earn good points like Brando and Ms. Ferguson?

He kept walking. After a few steps, he saw the figure of a woman walking in front of him. He did not know her. The woman stopped and turned around to face him.

"Joe, I am your mother, Kiesha!" she said. He was astonished to meet her for the very first time.

"Mother, is that really you?" Joe asked in total amazement.

"Yes, it's me, Joe."

"I've never met you. Growing up, I wanted to know where you were and why you left me alone."

"I was very young and confused when I gave birth to you. I was only sixteen. I didn't know what to do," she said, shaking her head.

"I was told you left me by a fire station one cold winter evening. Is that true?

"That's true, Joe. I wrapped you in the only warm coat I had. I shivered in that cold all night."

"But why, Mother? Why did you leave me there? I could have grown up to be a good son to you. Did you know I got the Distinguished Service Cross?"

"Yes, my son, I know. I was there that day when the secretary pinned the medal on you."

"How did you die, Mother?"

"I killed myself, Joe."

"How did you do that?"

"I took a full bottle of rat poison. Yes, it was painful, but it quickly ended my miserable life."

"What made you do it?"

"I felt I was a loser, Joe. I was an alcoholic prostitute in my teen years. There was no one to guide me, so I decided to kill myself."

"I was filled with so much anger at you, Mother, but now I understand you. Thank you for loving me. You must have known that I wanted to kill myself too."

"Yes, Joe, I knew. I knew you would suffer the same fate that I did. So I picked Ms. Ferguson and Brando to guide you. I prayed so hard, Joe, that you would meet inspiring people like them. And thank God you did! Unluckily, they moved out of your life too soon or else they would have guided you through."

"How about my father? Is he dead too?"

"No, Joe, that asshole of a father is still alive. Forgive my unkind words." She smiled at Joe. "And you will cringe when I tell you who he is."

"Who is he?"

"His name is Joe also. I was so in love with him that I named you after him."

"You said he is still alive?'

"Yes. He is in prison, but he's due to be out in seven months."

"What was he in for?"

"He was a drug and gun dealer on the streets. Sadly, Joe, he was the one who sold the gun that killed Ms. Ferguson and the drugs that killed Brando."

"Oh my God!" Joe was stunned by this news.

"But he has repented for his sins in prison. He is old now and he needs you, Joe."

"But I'm dead, just like you."

"No, Joe, you will come out of this alive. That bomb that Aliah detonated on both of you killed her but not you."

"Are you serious?"

"Yes, I was told that you will come out of this alive. I thank God, Joe, that you have this second chance at life."

"What happened to Aliah? Will I to see her again?

"Unfortunately, her body was dismembered, and she cannot be put back together. If she had died and her body was intact, she might have had a second chance like you." They had now reached the end of the tunnel where the bright light was coming from. Joe could see the blue sky and green mountains outside, and he felt the fresh ocean breeze.

"Good-bye, Joe, my one and only son. Always be assured that I love you and that my heart will always guide you." She hugged Joe, kissed him on his cheek, and then faded away on the dark side of the tunnel.

When the smoke cleared, Joe regained consciousness. He felt he was on a moving vehicle as he was being airlifted into an army helicopter. The attending army medic spoke to him.

"Joe, wake up! Thank God you're alive!"

Still unstable from his near-death experience, he responded in slurred words. "Where am I?"

An army medic with the Red Cross symbol on his helmet said, "You're in a helicopter, Joe. We're taking you to a military hospital." The helicopter made a sudden thrust before lifting off the ground. Joe looked down and saw mounds of war rubble almost everywhere on the landscape. Feeling a bit disoriented in the gliding craft, he asked the medic a question.

"I survived the bomb?"

"Yes, Joe, you're alive!" replied the medic, with a comforting smile on his face.

"Thank you, God!" He looked up to the clouds, thankful and relieved. The word *peace*, so elusive in this war-torn part of the world, struck him. He knew he had to reach out to his aging father to make peace with him, just as his mother had suggested. He planned to show his medal to his dad to make him proud. He touched his chest, but the medal was not there.

"Joe, you had a couple of shrapnel hit your leg and waist, but most of the bomb's shrapnel hit the army cross on your chest!" The medic pulled out the medal from his canvas medicine bag and showed it to Joe.

"What?" Joe could not believe what he was hearing. He recalled all the events that had happened from the time he had made the decision to take his own life until now: his heroism in battle, the bomb detonating with Aliah, and the life-threshold conversations with Ms. Ferguson, Brando, and especially his mother, Kiesha.

Holding the medal to show Joe, the medic had to explain his fate. "Look, Joe, this is your Distinguished Service Cross. The medal is now mangled and twisted because the shrapnels that were meant to kill you hit it instead!" Both of them were shaking their heads in disbelief.

"Joe, the cross saved your life!"

A CLEVER EMBEZZLER

I t was the first day of Yom Kippur, the Jewish Day of Atonement. For two days, devout Jews all over the world put their lives on hold to contemplate positive life changes and vow to follow them. The Jewish men and women that worked for Manhattan Stone Gems Inc. took this holiday seriously. None of them were working that day. The only employee working on this holiday was Ravi, who called himself a "liberal Hindu." He was the only non-Jew on the senior staff. For nine years now, Ravi had been the sole employee at the company during Yom Kippur and other Jewish holidays. As the Jews atoned for their sins and celebrated the start of their new year, Ravi worked alone. He didn't get any overtime pay either; it was just a regular workday for him.

As Ravi slid his ID card on the front-door pass, he was careful not to glance directly at the entrance's security camera. He also wore dark eyeglasses. He opened the door and put his coffee cup and two empty backpacks on his desk. He then sat down, turned his computer on, looked around the office somewhat nervously, and took a deep breath. His anxiety at that moment was quite elevated, even though he had planned every detail for the day methodically and meticulously for the last two years. Everything, he thought, must work flawlessly.

Ravi Patel was born in Mumbai, India, a city noted for the contrasting and flourishing jewelry stores and the widespread, overpopulated slum areas. His father was an employee of the railway transportation system, and his mother was a hardworking housewife. The family had three children. Ravi was the middle child. His ambitions were evident early on. He used to help his father clean the train interiors in the summer, getting paid pennies on the rupee and running with his broom from one railcar to the next. He had been a diligent student too. His recurring dream had been to get an education and go far away from the stench and squalor of the slums that his family had lived in for most of their lives.

He'd graduated with a finance management degree, hoping he would one day wear suits, shirts, and ties to work in the financial capital, New Delhi. He eventually did work there but only after working for five years for a diamond and precious-stones dealer in Mumbai. He got to know the precious-stones business quite well.

One day, his older sister was accepted to teach math and science at a high school in Queens, New York. Ravi's work ambitions shifted then, and he began to want to work at Wall Street in New York. But he felt that, for so many reasons, Wall Street was not ready to hire him. His thick Indian accent was one reason, and his spicy body scent was another. From Wall Street, he continued to walk southeast until he reached the diamond district. Once there, he was hired on the spot at Manhattan Stone Gems Inc. Still unmarried at thirty-two years old, he was sure this was the company that would someday make him rich.

Menachem, the owner of Manhattan Stone Gems, was not planning to hire a non-Jew and a nonrelative at that time. It was a business bound by trust and secrecy. But he needed someone who knew the precious-stones business well and had the dexterity and acuity to work on computers, which Ravi had proved he had. Menachem had been impressed by this naive but smart Indian fellow. He also knew that Ravi's sister worked in the city's public-school system, which led him to attribute much trustworthiness and respect to Ravi. He hired Ravi immediately.

The block of New York City's 47th Street between Fifth and Sixth Avenues is known worldwide as the diamond district and is one of the primary centers of the global diamond industry. The district grew in importance when Nazi Germany invaded the Netherlands and Belgium, forcing many Orthodox Jews to flee the diamond enclaves of Antwerp and Amsterdam and settle in New York City. Menachem and his family were descendants of those Orthodox Jews, and their business, Manhattan Stone Gems Inc., remained an active, major player in the industry.

The phone rang, and Ravi knew it was Menachem checking up on him.

"Hi, Ravi. Is everything there okay?"

"Yes, boss. I've got my breakfast and lunch so I don't have to go out. I'll be here until closing."

"Good. Don't forget to process the credit-card payment of Mr. Avigdor of Atlanta; that's close to $77,000."

"Yes, I saw that. I'll do it right away." Then Ravi thought of something funny. "Hey, isn't that a great name, Avigdor of Atlanta?"

"Yes, it's quite a name. You'll get to meet him, because he's coming to our office in two weeks. He's a great guy; you'll like him."

"Sure, no problem."

"That's great, Ravi. The phones will start ringing soon. Take care of business today, okay, Ravi?"

"Okay, Menachem, make sure you atone for your sins."

Ravi heard his boss laugh out loud as he hung up the phone. It was an example of the usual workplace banter that the two had to have to reassure each other that everything was okay. The pleasantness of it took away some of Ravi's anxiety. He felt guilty instead, guilty about the greedy plan he was about to carry out. Once again, he reviewed his motives.

Menachem had not been a fair and just manager to Ravi. He was quick to give good-sized raises and bonuses to his employees that were family members, but he gave a mere pittance, almost nothing, to Ravi, who did most of the work in the office. Ravi had complained to Menachem that this failure to fairly compensate him was unjustified. He deserved better pay. He had tried to quit four times. But each time he had handed in his resignation, Menachem had given him a small raise, enough for him to change his mind and stay. Ravi's long-running discontent with Menachem had evolved into a calculated vendetta that was about to punitively unfold today.

Ravi knew that Menachem would be calling back around four thirty, right before he closed the office. Tense and nervous, he stood up, walked decidedly to the metal safe, and started executing his carefully conceived plan.

There was a security camera focused on the front metal door of the five-foot-tall safe. He turned that camera off along with another camera inside the safe. He then entered the combination to open it. He was trusted enough to know the combination. He could feel his heart pounding heavily and his pulse racing as he pulled down the lever to unlock it.

When the safe door opened, he saw the green bundles of neatly stacked one-hundred-dollar bills all waiting to be touched and re-owned by him. He then grabbed the two backpacks that he had brought in that day and proceeded to grab bundles of cash. Each bundle of one-hundred-dollar bills amounted to $10,000. He filled his backpack with those money bundles as though he was picking bananas from the grocery-store shelves. Ravi's anxiety was somehow diminished as he focused on filling his bags with the cash bundles. He was thinking ahead to his planned getaway. There was no turning back now. The two backpacks were filled in just ten minutes.

Cash has remained the best payment option for purchasing diamonds and other gemstones, especially from suppliers in Asia and Africa. Strict industry regulations have been known to restrict the smooth flow of trade, and cash makes it so much easier to run a business. These suppliers normally have agents who personally travel to deliver and receive the cash payments, which are then deposited to a bank and remitted to them.

Ravi then turned to the precious stones. There was a smaller safe inside the big safe that contained all the diamonds, gemstones, and precious metals. He picked the best-cut diamonds, admiring their brilliance and sparkle under the florescent light. He took out a small leather bag from his pocket and put all the small-cut diamonds into it. He figured that the smaller sizes would be easier to sell and dispose of than the big ones. He squeezed all the stones into his backpacks. Altogether, he estimated the total value of the cash and stones to be 30 million dollars. That was enough to allow him a safe getaway and live comfortably for the rest of his life, which was his main goal.

When he got all that he wanted, he closed both safes and turned the security cameras on as though nothing had happened. He kept the backpacks out of camera view. At around one o'clock, after he had calmed his pumped-up adrenaline and composed himself, he telephoned Menachem.

"Hi, Menachem."

"Hi, Ravi, what's up?"

"I processed that credit-card payment from Avigdor of Atlanta. It was good."

"Very good. Are you busy there?"

"Not busy at all. I've had one phone call and that's it."

"If it's not too busy, maybe wait another couple of hours, and then you may leave early."

"I was going to suggest that too. Okay, I'll do that."

Everything was going well for Ravi so far. Menachem did not suspect a thing. Ravi thought of the money and gems as he looked at the backpacks behind the wall. They could buy him the best possible lifestyle for the rest of his life, and he would be free of any money worries. But what about his sister? Two years ago, Ravi's sister had gone back to Mumbai. She could not take the lazy, hostile attitude of the students in her class. It was at that time that Ravi came up with his plan to embezzle. All these thoughts were running through Ravi's head when the phone rang again. He picked it up to answer.

"Manhattan Stone Gems. Good afternoon."

"Yes, this is Avigdor; I'm from Atlanta. Did you get the payment I sent you?"

"Yes, Mr. Avigdor, I processed your credit-card payment this morning and it went through. I was just about to send you the receipt."

"That's exactly what I called about."

"Oh, I'm sorry, Mr. Avigdor! I was just busy. Do you want me to fax it or e-mail it to you?"

"Please e-mail it to me. My fax machine has not been working well."

"I will do it right away, sir!"

"Okay, thanks. By the way, my wife and I will be in New York in two weeks. Can you please ask Menachem to get us tickets for *The King and I*?

"That's a great show, sir. I know you'll love it. I will definitely tell Menachem to get you the theatre tickets."

"Very good. Uh, I don't think I got your name?"

"My name is Roby. Um, no, Ravi. Ravi." He'd accidentally slipped.

"Is it Roby or Ravi?" Avigdor was curious about the two names.

"Ravi. It is Ravi, sir."

"I can tell from your accent that you are from India. Am I right?"

"Yes, sir."

"How long have you worked with Menachem?"

"Nine years, sir."

"Okay, Ravi, it has been very pleasant talking to you. I'll see you in two weeks."

The smile on Ravi's face faded as he hung up the phone. He took a deep breath as he thought about how he had slipped and almost given up his cover, his would-be new name. He started to second-guess his decision. He had to ask himself, again, how long can I keep up the fake identity until I get caught? He glanced again at the two money-and-gemstone-filled backpacks neatly tucked behind the wall. Thirty million dollars will allow him to make a clean getaway and start a brand-new, carefree life. He just needed to be very, very careful.

Ravi did not wait for another hour to decide to leave. He picked up one backpack and slung it on his back, and then he picked up the other one and slung it on his front. He looked around the office one last time at the workplace he had been at for the past nine years. Then, with the firm resolve to change his life for the better, Ravi, determined and unwavering, walked out the door.

He stopped at his apartment. He changed his clothes, picked up the electric razor on his bed, plugged it in, and then stood in front of the mirror and started shaving his head bald. He did it neatly, allowing the shaved hair to fall not on the floor but only on the newspapers he had spread on the bed. After two minutes of shaving his head, he was completely bald. He gathered the newspaper spread, folded it up, and threw it into a black garbage bag. Then he took out his passport—a crisp, brand-new, fake passport with the official signature and stamps.

With a good, reliable Polaroid camera, he took a picture of his face—a serious, unsmiling face. He trimmed the edges of the picture to exactly fit the space on the fake passport. He then looked at the picture of this new person. He was bald and unsmiling, and he looked nothing like Ravi had ever looked before. Then, he read his new name.

Roby Motol was his new name. The first name Roby sounded similar to Ravi, and the last name Motol sounded similar to Patel. His new name sounded similar to his old one, so it should be an easy, effortless transition. But why the bald head?

Ravi had noticed that in a crowd, people do not stare at bald men. It's impolite. So, from now on, he would have to keep shaving his head to maintain its baldness and thus his anonymity.

He threw all of the other things he'd used—the shaver, the Polaroid camera, and the portable mirror—into the black plastic bag. He then emptied his two backpacks of their cash and gemstones, wrapped the valuable contents in black plastic bags, and set them neatly in a bigger, roller-wheeled canvas suitcase. That took a few minutes to do as he carefully made room for the cash and gemstones, clothes, and a good amount of his favorite Indian sausages. Yes, sausages.

He was panting and breathing heavily due to the weight of his luggage as he hailed a cab. When he got in, he said two words to the driver: "Penn Station." He threw away the black garbage bag at Penn Station, one of New York City's super-busy train stations, where he knew lots of garbage was generated and discarded every few hours. Then, breathing a sigh of relief, he waited for the train. It was here, as he waited in this public place, that he felt the pressures of being a fugitive. He looked over his shoulder often to see whether anyone was watching him. After waiting for about twenty minutes, he boarded the Silver Meteor train bound for Miami, Florida.

Nerves of steel. Ravi knew that in addition to his meticulous, clever planning, he would need nerves of steel to make a clean getaway. But the most daring part still remained—that is, the customs inspection. It was the last hurdle, the last piece of the plan he had to master, and one over which he had little control. Ravi knew that the cash and gemstones would show on the X-ray machines of both transport and Haitian customs inspectors.

How could he get all the money and gemstones past customs? This last part of his plan had taken the longest to figure out. In fact, he had almost abandoned the whole plan when he could not resolve this final part. The answer had finally fallen on him like heaven's grace when he'd met a fellow Indian named Akhil in Miami. It was Akhil who had seen him and spoken to him first. Akhil came from the town of Chemdur, a suburb of Mumbai about thirty miles from Ravi's home. They had not known each other growing up in India.

Akhil was a muscular twenty-seven-year-old with a wife and daughter in Chemdur who depended on him for support. He worked as a deckhand for the midsized cargo ships that navigated the ports of Miami and Cap-Haitien in Haiti. Resourceful and quick witted, Akhil saw himself as lucky to have found a good friend in Ravi. Trusting his new friend, he admitted to Ravi that he was in the country illegally. He sent most of earnings to his family, leaving just enough for him to survive. On his previous trips to Miami, Ravi had played a compassionate and generous older brother to Akhil, buying him good food and giving him money every time they met. Akhil was always happy and thankful to see Ravi. It did not take long for Ravi to ask Akhil a big favor regarding his very intimate luggage contents.

"Lamb Masala Sausage?" Akhil asked, very astonished.

"Yes! My aunt is in Port-au-Prince and Lamb Masala Sausage is her favorite, just as it is ours," Ravi answered with a straight face.

"And you want me to smuggle it onto the ship and into Haitian customs?"

"Yes, and my aunt is willing to pay you two hundred dollars for your efforts."

"Why don't you just declare it as a delicacy?"

"You know how strongly those sausages smell, don't you? With all the spices and curry inside of them? They will just throw them away." Ravi paused. "Lamb is very expensive, and I don't want them simply thrown away," he added.

"Okay, okay, I can do it. I have some very good friends in both ports who can help me. But I will have to inspect your luggage to make sure you're not bringing in drugs or explosives," Akhil cautioned.

"Sure! In the meantime, I will fly to Port-au-Prince, and I will be waiting for you in the port of Cap-Haitien," Ravi assured Akhil.

"Okay, but two hundred dollars is not enough for the risk I will be taking."

"Two fifty."

"Three hundred and not one penny less!"

"Okay, Akhil, you drive a hard bargain. My aunt will be thrilled."

Back at his New York apartment earlier, after he'd shaved his head bald for his fake passport, Ravi had taken all the loot from the two backpacks and wrapped the cash bundles and gemstones in three layers of thick, black plastic bags. He'd then wrapped them with his clothes and fitted them into a new, larger, one-piece rolling suitcase. Next, from his refrigerator he had brought out twenty-four pounds of Lamb Masala Sausage, which was wrapped in three-pound packages. He'd sprayed the frozen sausage packages with women's perfume to counter the smell. The backpacks were thrown out together with the other garbage. His new suitcase was the best smelling one of all.

As Ravi had planned, Miami was just a short stop. In Miami, he gave his perfumed luggage to Akhil, who took it as his own and boarded the mid-sized cargo ship on which he worked as a deckhand. The ship was bound for the port of Cap-Haitien, Haiti. Haiti is where Ravi planned to stay awhile and lay low. His dark skin would blend quite well there, he thought. With its well-known mass poverty and devastated infrastructure from natural calamities, Haiti was not the favorite port of call for embezzlers. So many stupid embezzlers, he thought, run to such exotic places like Brazil, Mexico, and

Switzerland, wanting to spend their ill-gotten loot right away, only to fall into the hands of the waiting police. That's how they get caught. Haiti was the last place the investigators would look, Ravi believed. His luggage went past an undisclosed side door with Akhil and past Haitian customs inspectors smoothly.

At the appointed time, the two Indian friends made their rendezvous at the port of Cap-Haitien. Akhil's face was grim and humorless as he confessed to Ravi, saying, "I took the liberty of taking all the Lamb Masala Sausage for myself, because you really don't need them."

"Okay, sure." Ravi looked at Akhil's piercing eyes with a questioning gaze.

"I saw all the things you were carefully hiding in your luggage, Ravi. You don't have to do this," Akhil said, wanting to change Ravi's plans.

"It's too late, Akhil. I already took some very big risks."

"It's not too late, Ravi. You can always turn back and return all of it." He looked at Ravi, seeking signs of remorse but seeing none. He persisted.

"Look, Ravi, we both grew up poor in Mumbai. Of course we want to get rich someday but not this way!" Akhil tried again to put some good sense into his guilty friend. "Think of your family, Ravi. Think of the shame and dishonor they will suffer in all of Mumbai!" Akhil said.

"It's too late, Akhil. It's too late." Unmoved by Akhil's plea, Ravi picked some cash out of his pocket to stop Akhil from getting into his conscience. "Here, Akhil, five hundred dollars for your efforts." He handed the cash to Akhil.

"Three hundred is good, Ravi. That's what we agreed on." He gave two hundred dollars back to Ravi. "I am now guilty of being an accessory to your crime." Akhil said, shaking his head.

"Don't worry, Akhil, I will never report you to immigration."

"I don't know if we will ever meet again, Ravi." Akhil looked at Ravi with very sad eyes.

"Thank you, Akhil, and good luck to you." The two hugged each other with heavy hearts. Then they parted ways.

It would be another five-hour bus ride from the port of Cap-Haitien to Port-au-Prince. Ravi had previously rented a room in the Port-au-Prince suburb of Petionville, a hilly section in the southern part of the Massif de la Selle mountain chain. Petionville was in the wealthier part of Haiti, where lots of American grocery items were available. The big earthquake of 2010 did some damage to the town, but with its wealthier population, it was quick to rebuild.

On his past trips to his Petionville, Ravi had slowly furnished his small apartment. He'd bought a small, heavy metal safe and placed it next to his bed at the far end of the room. He had a small, hotel-sized refrigerator, a one-coil burner electric stove, and a small flat-screen TV. All these were in place when he arrived this time with the loot. He didn't need anything else.

He arrived at his rented room at eleven o'clock at night. He brought out the paper bag with the cheeseburger and fries he'd bought at the airport and ate it quickly; he was tired and hungry. After emptying his luggage and putting the money and gemstones in the safe, he locked the safe securely and then took a long, cold shower. Only then did he feel calm and relaxed. He was now home safe. Whew!

Most of the news in Haiti was in Creole, the national language. There was an English news broadcast on TV at ten o'clock in the evening. On that broadcast the next day, there was a thirty-second news flash about a big embezzlement case in the diamond district of New York City. It mentioned that the estimated amount of currency and precious stones missing was $50 million. Ravi was stunned at the inflated valuation. The correct amount as per his recent count was only $30 million. He knew he had to stay in Port-au-Prince a little longer.

After three months of staying mostly indoors, Ravi grew restless. He wanted to cautiously and discreetly go out and roam about town. He'd noticed there were some Indians in this town because he'd heard them speaking. He would walk at the open markets and hear them speak their language. As much as he wanted to engage in their conversations, he would ignore them, pass them by, and pretend he was not one of them. The more he ignored them, the more he missed Indian food, jokes, and laughter. He felt he would have to come out more into the open soon.

After six months, Ravi was running out of gourdes, the Haitian currency. A dollar was equivalent to sixty-two gourdes at that time. He'd been able to save a lot of gourdes before, and those had been waiting for him in his safe. But now he had very little remaining. There were places such as banks and five star hotels where he could go and change his dollars into gourdes, but those places were filled with security cameras, which he knew he had to avoid. He could also try the active black market, which gave a slightly higher rate but could be dangerous. With all his dollars in the safe that he could not spend, he felt like he was floating on water and desperately dying of thirst at the same time. But like an adroit, nimble fox, Ravi always came up with an idea.

Ravi's laundry was being done by a lady named Delphine, who was a single mother with two sons, Andre, who was eight, and Armand, who was ten. Delphine's unmarried younger sister, Teres, lived with them too. Delphine was forty years old and a widow. Her husband was a hospital worker who died responding to the victims of the big earthquake when it hit. Delphine and Teres, who was thirty-three years old, did whatever kind of work they could find to put the two boys through school and, most importantly, food on the table. Ravi admired their hard work, and he would give them added tips for the neatly pressed clothes. Even the two boys would help with the laundry. Unbeknownst to them, Ravi was observing their good work ethic.

One afternoon he spoke to them of his plan. "I want to start a business, and I want all four of you to work for me," Ravi said to them in the best Creole he could speak. They were interested.

"What kind of business?" Delphine asked.

"I'd like to sell food, hot dogs and hamburgers only, with just one drink, cold pineapple juice." Ravi waited for their reaction. They became excited. "Do you think those foods will sell well?" he asked. They all nodded their heads and smiled in agreement. They were definitely excited.

"Oh, they will sell very well! Everybody likes them!" Delphine answered. But then she asked, "Where will your store be?"

"Our store," Ravi began, and they grew even more excited when they heard those words, "will be at the open public market. I will buy everything you need: the grills, the turners, the cups, the ice, and, of course, the meat and drinks. I will also give you a good salary."

"When do we start?" Teres asked quite anxiously.

"I'm getting a used van tomorrow so I can buy everything we need. We'll start business the next day!"

They all hugged Ravi and promised him that they would work very hard for him.

It was the only way to utilize his hundred-dollar bills. Ravi would pay the suppliers with his hundred-dollar bills, and he knew they would accept them with no questions. He would, in turn, have all the gourdes from the business sales. It was money laundering, pure and simple. He would also be helping a family of four make enough money for their needs. Ravi was excited about his clever idea.

Ravi bought the used van with cash and, together with his four new employees, set up the grill at the open public market. Then he bought the tools, the meats, a good supply of canned pineapple juice, the charcoal, and the blocks of ice. They were in business.

When Ravi saw the long lines of customers leading to his small store, he was amazed. He was now an entrepreneur, a dream he had nurtured for some time. He never thought his dream business would come together in Haiti. And as long as he was managing hardworking, honest employees, he vowed to himself he would always treat them fairly, giving them part of the profits with bonuses. But wait! What if they embezzled money from him, just like he had done to Menachem? It was a risk he could not allow. He would have to keep a very close watch on the money and merchandise. Meanwhile, the long lines to his store continued day after day.

About six months later, Delphine and Teres wanted to speak to him. "Our customers are asking for more food choices, Roby," Delphine reported.

"Yes, Roby, they want chicken sandwiches, French fries, bacon and tomatoes with their hamburgers, and, also, ice cream. They also want tables and chairs, just like McDonald's," Teres seconded.

"I wish I could price them like McDonalds." He stopped to think, and then he responded, saying, "Okay, we'll give them what they want." Ravi then cautioned the women. "But with the added food, you will be busier."

"No problem, Roby, my boys give us much help after school. They are strong and hardworking. They like the money they make," Delphine assured him. And the business grew even more.

It had now been a year and three months since Ravi had begun his embezzlement journey. The last reward Ravi saw offered on television for information leading to the diamond-district embezzler was two million, and that was two months ago. Lately, there had been no more mention of the New York City cash and stones robbery in the news. Ravi thought his trail must have gone cold for investigators. It was time to move again. He needed to be several steps ahead of them.

Asia and South Africa were the places he had researched that he could go next to hide. They were also the places he could unload and get the most money for the precious stones. But the more he thought about it, the more he was convinced that Petionville was the best place for him to stay. He now spoke Creole, his business was thriving, and, despite the constant fear of being caught, he was living a great carefree life. He liked the cool, breezy hills of Petionville and its polite, friendly people. He had also become very fond of the pretty and virtuous Teres.

Teres was that woman with the shy smile, Ravi noticed right away. He knew that a lot of male customers came to their store just so they could be waited on by Teres. She was honest and charming. She had remained unmarried to help her sister make a living. When Delphine was widowed, she vowed to help her and her two sons. Ravi was attracted to Teres's dedication to her family and her deep personal ambition.

The two went out on a date one evening. Ravi had planned a surprise for Teres, something totally unpredicted.

"Have I been a good person to you, Teres?" Ravi asked softly, with a tender smile on his face.

"Oh, Roby, you have been the most generous boss I have ever worked for," Teres replied truthfully. "Why do you ask?"

"I believe I have fallen in love with you, Teres," he said, his voice nervously cracking a bit. He continued. "I have been watching you from afar with great affection and admiration. I like the way you smile, the way you work, and the simple way you dress," he said and paused to swallow. "I really love you, Teres!"

Teres was not ready for those frank words of affection that evening, but she could feel the warmth of Ravi's well-chosen lines. "Roby, I don't know what to say!"

Ravi pulled out a small red box from his pocket, opened it, took a deep breath, and said the words with an audible whisper. "I love you, Teres, and, with this ring, I want you to marry me!"

Teres had tears when she saw the ring. It was the first time she had seen a beautiful, sparkling ring like that. She wiped her tears with her hands. Ravi took her right hand and slipped the ring onto her hardened, callous-filled finger. Teres could not believe that emotional moment. She quickly made her decision.

"Yes, Roby, yes! I will marry you!" She was smiling, with tears flowing down her cheeks as they hugged tightly. Roby had tears as well. Teres was his first true love.

"Just don't hurt me, Roby. Promise me you won't hurt me!" Teres made him swear. "I am not rich, not even educated. All I want is to live with you in dignity!" she tearfully pleaded.

"I will never hurt you, Teres." He swore with his right hand up. They continued to talk until the early hours of the next day, just like lovebirds. They could not stop talking of their future. For all their honest talk, Ravi did not tell Teres about the embezzlement.

Ravi took Teres back to her home at about two in the morning. The night was filled with abounding promises as they both planned for their forthcoming wedded life after years of prolonged singlehood. Ravi drove home, parked his business van at the usual place, and walked the eight yards to his apartment. From a dark corner, he heard his name called.

"Ravi Patel!"

He turned around to look. Four men grabbed him and threw him to the ground facedown. Then they identified themselves.

"FBI, Mr. Patel, you are under arrest for grand larceny, tax evasion, and illegal possession of stolen property and currency!"

Ravi was powerless. He spoke in surrender, saying, "Okay, okay!"

"My name is Special Agent Gary Carson, Mr. Patel, you know that everything you say can and will be used against you in a court of law!"

"Yes, I know! I want to tell you that all the money and stones I stole are in my safe in my apartment."

"Where?" asked Agent Carson.

"In my apartment," Ravi answered.

Carson turned his radio phone on and spoke to another FBI agent. "Bill, Mr. Patel said there is a safe in his apartment. Did you see it?" After a few minutes, the other agent replied. "No safe in this apartment,

Gary." Ravi insisted on going to the apartment, but no safe was found there.

That same morning, Ravi was extradited to New York City. He was sentenced to seven to ten years in prison and ordered to pay back the amount he had embezzled, the full thirty million dollars, as restitution.

Two weeks of prison life passed. Ravi had some time to accept that his clever plans were not as clever as he had thought. He could be seen shaking his head and talking to himself, trying to figure out what went wrong. His bright-orange prison suit made him think of all the suits and nice clothes he was planning to buy with the embezzled cash. He could not believe his fate.

One morning Ravi was informed that he had a male visitor. He did not recognize the man until he identified himself.

"Hi, Ravi. My name is Avigdor, and I'm from Atlanta. Do you remember me?"

"Hi," Ravi reluctantly replied.

"I used to work for Israeli intelligence, the Mossad. But I'm retired now," he told Ravi. Avigdor looked and sounded commanding with his brawny arms and neck and robust tone of voice.

"I am now in the precious-stones business, Ravi, and I also do recovery of stolen property for the industry."

Ravi was stunned. He could not speak.

"You know, Ravi, you should have changed your mind about stealing the money and gemstones when you blew your fake name to me. Remember you told me your name was Roby and then changed it to Ravi?"

Ravi nodded his head slightly, not wanting to acknowledge the slip. Avigdor went on.

"I had my suspicions about you right after we spoke on the phone, so I called Menachem immediately. He checked the security cameras using his cell phone and said everything looked okay. He trusted you." Avigdor paused and then said, "Remember it was Yom Kippur. We Jews were not supposed to do any kind of work. He discovered the missing cash and gemstones two days later, after the holidays." He paused and then continued. "You timed it very well, Ravi. That gave you lots of time to flee."

Ravi was uncomfortable but wanted to know more.

"You had a good escape plan. Your trail had gone cold. We could not find you anywhere." Avigdor smiled admiringly.

"How did you know where I was then?" Ravi asked very curiously.

"Your friend Akhil called us when he heard about the reward money."

Ravi looked up, not quite stunned. He had known Akhil was aware of his embezzlement. In fact, whenever he heard about the reward money, he was worriedly reminded of Akhil.

Avigdor went on. "But Akhil did not know where in Haiti you'd be hiding." He paused to smile. "But when you bought the ring at the jewelry store, the woman recognized you from the television news and called our number."

Ravi was shaking his head. He should have known better.

"Menachem is the big winner here. He collected from his insurance company for his loss, and he got the money and gemstones from your safe." He paused again with a broader grin. "In fact, Ravi, Akhil is now working for Menachem, doing your old job." He stopped smiling and felt sorry for the repentant Ravi.

It was a big punch in the gut knowing there was no way he could go back to Menachem even if he sought forgiveness. But Ravi was curious. "How did Menachem get the contents of my safe?"

"Two of my bounty hunters had carried it out earlier, before the FBI arrived." Avigdor smiled again. "Menachem instructed me to give all the gourdes to Delphine and Teres. They were very happy to receive it; it was about a quarter of a million gourdes."

Tearfully, Ravi asked Avigdor about his love. "Did Teres say anything about me?"

"Oh yes, she said she will be waiting for you. She promised." He paused and then said, "She told me she fell in love with you even before you proposed to her." Avigdor smiled again. "Teres will be writing to you. I gave her your address. Make sure you write back to her, huh, Ravi?" He stood up to leave and gave Ravi a friendly, consoling tap on the shoulder. "You're still a winner, Ravi!"

Outwitted, outsmarted, and definitely outclevered, Ravi realized that his embezzlement plans were not that clever after all. Not at all. Menachem and Akhil, he imagined, would be pleasantly having coffee with each other in the diamond district at this moment, joking with each other and laughing hard at him now that he was in jail. He, the supposed clever one, should have heeded Akhil's advice to turn himself in and surrender his embezzlement loot. But he did not. He chose to ignore Akhil's timely brotherly advice. Blinded by his supposed cleverness, nothing could have persuaded him to go back.

Ravi watch as Avigdor slowly walked away and faded behind the steel prison doors. He was now resigned to patiently serving his jail term, one day at a time. His clever plans were over. His family from Mumbai had not contacted him yet. They were probably shocked at the embezzler he had turned out to be. His eyes stayed fixed on the door, which he knew he would be walking out of in about five years, with good behavior. With a slight, expectant smile on his face, he thought of going back to Haiti, where his faithful Teres would be waiting, as she had faithfully promised.

WARAY-WARAY NURSE

*"I would rather die a meaningful death
than live a meaningless life."*

—*Corazon C. Aquino*

I t was an exhausting night shift for Linda Santos
and the emergency room crew at the Catholic hospital, one of eight trauma centers in the state. The
exhausting and emotionally unnerving shift stuck
with Linda as she drove home, her mind focused on
the kind of trauma case she had hoped she'd never
ever see or be a part of again.

The trauma call had come at 7:25 last night. The
evening Emergency Room crew had just started their

shift when their beepers sounded. "Trauma alert, juvenile gunshot," was the beeper message. "Juvenile gunshot" were the words Linda dreaded most. Right away she thought of her nine-year-old twins, Kieran and Kayla, who were at home with their father, Linda's husband, Crispin, and were supposedly doing their homework. Within ten seconds of the beeper sound, the hospital loudspeaker repeated the worrying message, "Trauma alert, juvenile gunshot, fifteen minutes!"

Like they were trained to do, the ER response team leaped into action. Each one of them grabbed a disposable, protective green paper gown and wore it with the Velcro link in the back. Then they put on latex gloves and the protective face mask that covered their mouths and noses. The technician wheeled his mobile X-ray machine and stood by the door of the ER station. The hospital chaplain came in and started praying for the unnamed juvenile, seeking God's almighty power to save the victim. Linda managed to take out her cell phone and dial her home number.

"Yes, Linda?"

"Cris, are you all okay?"

"Yes we're okay. Are you okay?"

"We're getting a juvenile gunshot victim in a few minutes. The shooting happened in the town next to ours. I just wanted to make sure you're all okay."

"Yes, we heard the ambulance siren about five minutes ago. The shootings have become all too common, huh?"

"Yes, they have. I thought of the kids right away."

"Don't worry, we're all okay. They are just finishing their homework. They ate all the eggrolls you made, and Kieran even ate more.

"Let me talk to him."

A familiar child's voice spoke on the phone. "Hi, Mom. I only ate one eggroll more than Kayla, and she said I was unfair!"

Then a young girl's voice spoke on the phone. "Mom, there was one extra eggroll, and Kieran grabbed it and ate it right away. He should have shared it with me like a good brother. Right, Mom?"

"Well, I'll make sure to make more tomorrow, and I will make it an even number so you don't feel cheated. Bye for now; I have to work." Linda heard the emergency room automatic glass door open and saw four paramedics come in, hurriedly wheeling in a young man with his head heavily bandaged.

"Bye, Mom!" Linda did not get to answer her daughter on the phone. She immediately sprang into emergency mode.

The paramedics rushed the young victim to the waiting-station bed as the doctors and nurses tried to stabilize the bleeding. The senior paramedic loudly read the stats he had gathered: "Victim's name is Andrew Smith, African American male, ten years old, with an entry gunshot wound on the right cheek. BP is ninety over sixty and dropping, pulse eighty and fading fast. The bullet is still in the victim." The doctor attached an oxygen mask to the patient as Linda set the intravenous liquid in his vein and another nurse placed gauze on the open wound to stem the bleeding.

"Take him to the OR immediately!" the attending doctor instructed.

Linda set the I.V. fluid on the pole hook and was ready to stay behind when the young victim grabbed her thumb tightly. He wouldn't let her go. It was a common reaction in a subconscious patient to grab on to a nurse. Linda had to go with the patient to the OR.

The victim was wheeled to the operating room as the chaplain walked briskly with the team, praying continuously. The ER doctor who was left behind could not help but ask the paramedic, "How did this happen?"

"From what we've gathered, the three boys were playing basketball in the victim's driveway when a car drove by and fired shots in their direction."

"Who were the gunmen?"

"That's what the police are working on."

The ER doctor threw his hands in the air in total frustration, saying, "Why can't we ever control guns?"

The O.R. surgeons and the nurses' team were ready and waiting for the young victim. Linda had to take his grip off her hand as the OR team worked on him. The bloody gauze on his cheeks was filling up with blood. It was one hospital shift Linda would never forget. The young victim was about the same age as her twin kids.

Linda's shifted ended at seven in the morning. Their family routine worked like this: she'd get home, and the kids would be gone to school, having been dressed and fed by her husband, Cris, a plant engineer, who'd be gone to work. Linda would then have a light breakfast and sleep during the day. It was the routine that they had to follow so that both of them could work. But this morning, as much as she tried to, she could not sleep.

The image of that young shooting victim, with his bloody, battered young face and his total helplessness, would not leave her. His desperate grip on Linda's finger had told her that he'd been trying hard to stay alive. Linda tossed and turned in her bed, with the shift's events playing over again in her head. Yesterday's patient was the ninth juvenile shooting victim in Linda's seven years in the ER. There had been many adult shooting victims that had gone through the ER, but the young, innocent kids didn't deserve to die from adult gun violence. She looked at the picture of her twins on her bedside table, and she prayed. "God, please protect my family, especially my children. Do not allow any kind of harm to come to them. We love them dearly, as I know you do too. Keep them safe when Cris and I are not around to look after them. They are the best life blessings you have given Cris and I, and I pray, dear God, that you will shield them from harm and gun violence, against which they have no defense at all. Amen."

Linda felt better after that short prayer. She closed her eyes and hoped she would finally fall asleep. Then their neighbor's dog started barking again. Normally, her tired body from the twelve-hour shift puts her to sleep despite the dog's barking. But not this morning. She got up and walked down to the kitchen and poured herself a glass of milk. She took out a pen and a piece of blank white bond paper and sat down to write a letter. The words in the letter had been sitting in her mind for some time, perhaps since she had started tending to juvenile gunshot victims. It was a letter she believed strongly that she had to write.

To the Editor
The Washington Post
1301 K Street NW
Washington, DC 20071

Dear Editor:
   My name is Erlinda Santos, I have been a hospital emergency room nurse for seven years. During this period, I have given urgent

emergency care to juvenile gunshot victims. So far, during my shift, there have been nine young victims brought to us due to gunshot wounds. I know there have been many more, and, regrettably, there will be many more to come. Five of the victims died from those unintended, indiscriminate bullets. The other four miraculously survived but with permanent scars that remind them every day of the tragedies brought about by guns.

Why can't we control guns, Mr. Editor? I do not understand. Our lawmakers are quick to regulate airlines when they overcharge us or pharmaceutical companies when their products report early negative side effects. Why can't they write laws that will limit gun availability for those unfit to use them, such as gang members, the mentally ill, and, most dreaded of all, radical terrorists? Are gun manufacturers so powerful that they are able to control lawmakers' insecurities to their advantage?

My husband and I have two children. They are nine-year-old twins, and they will be celebrating their birthdays next month. They are so excited that they will be ten years old, the age when they think they know most of everything. Unfortunately, that is the same age at which an innocent boy died today at our hospital due to a senseless gun-shot wound.

I don't know much about making laws, Mr. Editor. My job as a nurse is to save lives and get them back to normal. I have witnessed many lives lost due to guns, and I cannot stay silent anymore. My frustrations, and those of the others I work with, have reached an unbearable level. That is the reason why I wrote you this letter. Guns continue to kill young innocent victims.

Should our insecure lawmakers need help in drafting gun-control laws, I am willing to take some time to share my experiences as a nurse to help them do that. Better yet, maybe my almost-ten-year-olds can help them. It is simple common sense.

Respectfully,
Erlinda Santos

Linda felt good after writing the letter. Her frustration had abated a bit. Writing those words highlighting gun-control urgency, with the mild dose of sarcasm, gave her a much-needed sense of unleashed accomplishment. She folded the letter, put it in her desk drawer, and went to sleep.

Linda and Cris come from the Philippine province of Samar, one of the largest provinces in the country and part the Eastern Visayan region. The people of Samar are called *Waray*, which translates to "none" or "nothing," due to their sense of contentment with whatever they have. The people speak the Waray-Waray dialect, one of the nineteen officially recognized regional languages in the country. The Waray people are stereotyped as brave warriors, an image popularized by the phrase "Basta Waray, hindi uurong sa away" ("Warays never back down from a fight"). This historically earned bravado is tempered by their Christian religion. They are some of the most devout Roman Catholics in the Philippines.

Linda, now a nurse supervisor, was a smart health-care practitioner who had moved up the ranks primarily due to her good work ethic. She had that caring attitude toward her patients, who have always thanked her for it and have written to the hospital commending her for her endearing warmth and humor. But she could be outspoken when fairness in the workplace was breached. She had reported a doctor's verbal abuses of new and timid nurses. She also politely questions some doctors' prescription orders when she feels she has to. This five foot tall, slightly heavyset nurse with dark brown skin and an ever-friendly smile, knows her life vocation.

The warmth and genuine care, the humor with patients, and the Waray-Waray outspokenness have together motivated Linda sufficiently that she has to take a stand on guns. Why can't lawmakers reconcile the responsible sale of guns with common-sense gun regulations? The answers that she gathered from her research were that

1. If the sale of guns is controlled, then down the road, gun owners might lose the right to bear arms as guaranteed by the second amendment of the Constitution.
2. Criminals will always have guns, and people have the right to protect themselves.

Linda's concerned conscience remains unconvinced that open access to guns is the answer. And the continued resistance by lawmakers to regulate guns makes the death toll grow every day.

As she continued to sleep soundly, Linda was taken over by a dream, a nice pleasant dream. Her family was taking a fun, leisurely day at an amusement park. The sun was out, the sky was blue, and children's laughter filled the air with playful screams. Her twins excitedly hopped on to the carousel, and her husband Cris held them both securely on their mounts as the carousel started to move with the rhythm of the pleasant children's music that was starting to play. Linda headed for the food kiosk at the next booth to get some popcorn, candy, and drinks for all of them. She was having fun seeing them having fun.

Then, the dream instantly turned dark and frightening. From out of nowhere, Linda saw a man wearing a dark-colored overcoat, unusual for a nice day like this. The man was Caucasian, with uncombed hair and a menacing, evil look in his eyes. She stood frozen for a moment and followed the man's movements as he headed for the carousel. The man reached the carousel and looked at the kids riding on the faster-moving mounts. Then, Linda saw the man bring out two handguns from his coat pocket. He had one gun in each hand. She turned and started running toward him, praying that she could stop him from firing even one shot. Running as fast as she could, she slipped on some melted ice cream in her path. Then she heard one shot fired as she fell on the dark-coated man, tackling him like a football player. She and the man both fell on the ground. She awoke on impact.

Sweating and screaming from that dream, she realized she was on her bed again and was thankful it was only a dream. She picked up the picture of her twins from her side table, kissed them, and cried. What a dream! Could it be a premonition, a warning of some tragedy about to happen to her family? Now, she is more determined than ever to be a gun-control advocate, a title she thought she would never have. A gun-control advocate. That's what she has now become.

Linda got up from her bed and walked in her pajamas to her desk. She took out the letter from the drawer and then turned on her computer. She was definitely sending her letter to the editor of the

Washington Post. There was no stopping this Waray. She could not just sit idly by and let gun regulations continue to stall, not anymore. This Waray nurse was mad as hell and could take it anymore. Linda typed the newspaper's e-mail address on the recipient line. On the subject line, she typed "A Concerned Nurse on Guns." With her heart pounding, her fingers trembling, and tears of anger and frustration boiling over from her ever-compassionate heart, she typed the words of her hand-drafted letter carefully, wanting to make her message clear, loud, and very readable. Then she clicked "Send."

It was a slow news day at the *Washington Post* at eleven o'clock that morning, but the opinion/editorial page editors were busy. One of the staff editors, Mark, was reviewing the letters that had come in from the fully loaded e-mails. One by one he perused the e-mail subjects of senders, trying to pick an interesting one and hoping he could get a read on the pulse of their readers that day. He stopped to look at one that caught his eye, "A Concerned Nurse on Guns." He opened it and read it slowly at first. Halfway through, he realized he had a good opinion letter, with words that leaped out from his screen. This letter—simple and sincere with an effective use of sarcasm—echoed the sentiments of the current headlines, he thought. He printed it and brought it to his boss.

"This has to be our lead editorial," Mark said as tried to convince his boss. "It's coming from a health-care professional directly impacted by gun deaths." His boss, who was impressed by the cleverly written letter, agreed with Mark. "Go ahead, Mark, put it on top," he said. The next day, Linda's letter was the lead editorial in the influential *Washington Post.*

Two days later, Linda was awakened by a call on her cell phone. It was her husband calling from his workplace.

"Ma, did you write to the *Washington Post?*"

"Yes, Dad. Why? Did you read it?

"Yes, I am reading it right now."

"I did not know they were going to read it, much less publish it."

"Well, they published it. It was the first letter on the opinion pages." Cris sounded disappointed.

"Please bring it home; I want to see it."

"Why did you not tell me you were going to write to the *Post?*"

"Cris, I have cried to you about this. I could not take the deaths from guns anymore, especially of kids." Linda realized her mistake of not telling her husband. "I'm sorry, Pa!"

"Look, Ma, I understand what you wrote is your opinion, and you are free to say it, but do you know how big and powerful the gun lobby is?"

"Dad, I had a dream one day that a man, an evil-looking man, was about to shoot you and our kids. I could not let that happen, and I was scared that if

I didn't send the letter, that dream might just come true. It might happen!"

"Still, you should have discussed it with me first."

"Sorry, Pa, it was impulsive of me to—" The line went dead. Cris had hung up. He was upset.

Linda realized that Cris was right. Her letter could have unexpected effects that she had not given much thought to. She wished she hadn't sent the letter without consulting Cris. But there was no taking it back now; it was published. She just hoped Cris would be on her side of the issue.

The next day, Linda was coming home around eight o'clock in the morning. She parked her car on the driveway, opened the car door, and got out. Then she heard a man's voice call her name.

"Mrs. Erlinda Santos?" Two men, both of them about six feet tall and wearing similar light-colored, long-sleeved shirts, were walking toward her. Both were clean-cut, smiling, and friendly.

"Yes?"

"My name is Tom, and this is my friend Jerry," the blond guy said, introducing them both as they walked closer to Linda.

"What can I do for you?" Linda was worried. The two men were not carrying guns, but she was not sure of their intentions.

"Mrs. Santos, we just want you to know that the piece you wrote to the *Washington Post* about guns was upsetting to us," the dark-haired man said.

Linda stopped to face them. "Are you here to ha-rass me?" Linda asked, feeling a bit anxious. "That is my personal opinion, and I have the right to send it to the *Post*."

"We know that, Mrs. Santos. We are not here to harass you, just to inform you of our opinions on the issue as well." They both sounded pleasant, but their height and build were intimidating to Linda, and they knew that. It was their intent to intimidate her. She locked her car and went up to her porch; the two men did not follow.

Linda brought out her front-door keys from her pocket and opened the door. She went in and then quickly locked the door. The two men did not leave but instead stayed standing on her driveway. She called the local police number that was written near the phone. The lady on the phone said the police were coming. She looked out the window again, and the two men were still there.

There were no pedestrians on the neighbor-hood streets at that time. Their neighbors were all at work. The two guys must have known that, be-cause they were not leaving. She prayed that the po-lice would come right away, but there was no sign of them. Finally, she knew she had to do something. She opened their front door, which made the two men look at her. Then she went out, and, armed with a long, shining, sharp butcher knife, she yelled at them.

"You two guys are trespassing on my property!" she shouted at them as she held the butcher knife with her two hands and walked slowly toward the two. The men looked at each other and started to step back. Linda could smell the sudden fear on them. Initially the men were the "harassers," but they were now the "harassees." Linda walked a few steps toward them, brandishing the butcher knife and ready to use it. Tom and Jerry retreated hurriedly to their car, which was parked across the street, and sped away. Linda breathed a sigh of relief, an empowering relief.

Sunday was the twins' party. There were about twenty kids invited to the twins' birthday party. While the kids played in the backyard, the adults talked about the gun issue, each one voicing similar concerns. They had just finished singing the birthday song when the phone rang.

A man's voice said, "Hello, is this Mrs. Erlinda Santos?"

"Who are you?" Linda defiantly replied.

The soft-spoken voice answered, "Mrs. Santos, my name is Rabbi Thomas Klein. I hope I am not disturbing you."

"How can I help you, sir?" Linda became respectful but abrupt; she was very busy with her guests.

"There will be an anti-gun rally on the high-school grounds on Friday night. We read your editorial in the *Washington Post* and we'd really like you to speak about your concerns at the rally," the rabbi said.

Linda sat down, trying to pay better attention. She could not believe she was able to get people's attention with her letter. It was an issue she was willing to fight for. She asked, "What time on Friday night?"

"Seven o'clock."

"I am working that evening, but I'll see if I can find someone to cover for me."

"Thank you very much, Mrs. Santos. We'll see you on Friday."

Linda hung up the phone, a bit overwhelmed by the attention that her letter had gotten. She saw this as a chance to see how many people shared her gun concerns. The rally could start that much-needed grassroots awareness that could cause lawmakers to take notice. The Waray boldness in her was suddenly awakened, and she felt a greater sense of purpose. She was daringly excited. The people were waking up on this issue; she could not miss that rally. But what would Cris say?

"I know those young gun victims have given you reason to advocate for them; I also know that you are smart, and you will be a good person for this cause. There will be setbacks and frustrations in any revolution, Linda. I just pray to God that He will guide you and keep you safe so that you can achieve what we so desperately want." Cris kissed her and gave her a warm, loving embrace; they were now both in this advocacy together.

There were some fiery and passionate speakers at the gun-control rally, which had been sponsored by the PTA. The three pizzerias in town had donated the food and drinks. The businesses, the bankers, and the shop owners were all there, knowing that unregulated guns could hurt their businesses as well. When it was time for Linda to speak, she went up to the stage nervously, unaware of how people would react to what she had to say. Dressed in her scrubs, she slowly narrated the events of that night when she'd cared for a juvenile gunshot victim who had grabbed her thumb and held on to her all the way to the operating room. And despite her prayers with the chaplain, the ten-year old had died. Linda could not help but shed tears, and she saw tears in other people's eyes as well. The feisty, fighting Waray in her had now been launched and activated.

Linda appeared on the cover of the local newspaper with her arms raised in defiance, tears in her eyes, and her face exposing the deep frustration in her heart. It was the best picture that captured a nation's collective pain and exasperation over lawmakers' inaction on gun control. She had now become the face, the image, of the gun-regulation revolution, as the headlines boldly declared: "Nurse Fights for Gun Control." Linda had become an instant but reluctant celebrity. But not everyone agreed with her, and she expected that.

Linda was coming home from her twelve-hour shift one Saturday morning when she passed a dark-blue car parked on the street about one block from her house with the driver in it. When she parked her car in the driveway, she looked at the dark-blue car and noticed that the driver had long, light-colored hair and appeared to be female. She could not read the license plates from the distance, but Linda saw that the driver had her finger on her cell phone, covering her face. She stared at the driver for a few minutes to send the message that she was aware of her unwelcome, annoying presence and to show her that she was not afraid. But she was.

Linda rang their doorbell. She could hear the two kids running, each trying to be the first one to open the door. As the kids hugged and kissed Linda, she turned her head toward the direction of blue car. She saw the driver put her cell phone down and put her hand on the lower part of the steering wheel to start the car. The car moved slowly toward her house at first, and then it stopped right in front of her driveway. Linda saw the driver's gloved hand pick up a shiny metal object from the passenger's seat. She grabbed her two kids and tried to shield them from the possible gunshots. She was hit in the upper right shoulder. The blue car sped away.

Bleeding from her shoulder wound, Linda and her kids fell on the tiled floor. Cris, who was cooking the family breakfast, ran to the front door, shocked at the sight of the three. He helped Linda to a chair and grabbed a towel to stem the bleeding. The two kids were not hit. Neighbors came out of their houses after hearing the gunshots to see if Linda and the kids were okay. One couple rang her doorbell because they were so concerned. "Linda, Linda, are you okay?" they asked.

"We heard the gunshots, Linda! Are you okay?" asked an elderly lady. All of her neighbors walked up to her and hugged her, instinctively protecting her from anyone who would try to shoot at her again.

"I called the police. They are coming!" an elderly gentleman said.

"I'm okay, I'm okay!" she insisted, and she hugged her neighbors back, recognizing their bravery in coming out to try to protect her. It was the best show of support for her cause.

Linda was at the hospital when she saw next morning's newspaper headline. "Gun Control Activist Shot" it read. This apparent warning from her enemies was enough for Crispin and the kids to be concerned.

"Mom, do you think they will shoot us again at our house?" Kieran worriedly asked his mother.

"No, Kieran, don't let them scare you, son. I think they're just mad at me, not you," Linda answered calmly.

"I can't understand, Mom. You're only trying to protect innocent gun victims. Why are they mad at you?" Kayla asked, trying to make sense of the incident. It was Crispin who replied, a bit angry.

"Your mom touched some raw nerves, just like when someone touches an exposed electric wire and the lights then go out. I think your mom has touched that wire and the lights of those who disagree with her are starting to dim." It was a great example of an explanation from Crispin. Linda could not add any more to it, as it had calmed her children down. The couple remained at the dining table as the children went to bed.

"Are you angry at me, Cris, for getting into this mess?" She was ready to accept a tirade of negatives from her husband. Surprisingly, he remained calm.

"I have been thinking about how you got started with this gun issue," he said. "Those juvenile victims could have been rushed to the other hospitals, but instead most of them came to you, on your shift." Crispin touched Linda's hand and continued. "I believe this gun-control advocacy has been entrusted to you Linda, and we can expect more warnings from the enemy." He spoke with a soft voice, looking at Linda's eyes.

"You mean you're not mad at me for having caused this shooting?" Linda was surprised at her husband's calm response.

"Well, I am and I'm not," Cris said and then paused to take a deep breath. "I am concerned that they will come back and shoot at the kids; that would kill me and you." Again, he took a deep breath. "But then, you could be very close to gun-control legislation." The husband and wife sat quietly, unable to find the right words for the moment. Linda finally spoke.

"Someone suggested that I get a gun. You know, for protection." Linda tried to get his reaction.

"Someone suggested that to me too!" he said, placing his hands on his face as he pondered the suggestion.

"I'm afraid that the kids might find it, and I don't want to think of what could happen." Linda was scared of those possibilities. Cris nodded his head and said, "Let's think about it."

The couple received e-mails of concern from gun-control advocates like Michael Bloomberg, former mayor of New York City and owner of Bloomberg L.P., a vast business information network, and former congresswoman Gabby Giffords and her astronaut husband, Mark Kelly. With these big names behind her, she would now cross the path, and the ire, of the equally big and powerful Washington gun lobbyist John B. Cassfield.

John B. Cassfield graduated from law school magna cum laude. His impressive courtroom cross-examinations came from his years as a gifted college debater, where he was fierce, poised, and always convincing. He started practicing law as a state prosecutor, during which time he challenged the lawyers of some gun manufacturers. It was the gun industry who enticed him to cross over to their side as one of their attorneys. He then rose to the ranks as head lobbyist, handling both legal defense and congressional lobby for the gun industry. For this, he is generously compensated.

Worried that gun owners were closely identifying themselves with this diminutive Filipina nurse-turned-gun-control advocate and that they were losing their base support, John B. Cassfield sought a meeting with Linda. A closed, confidential meeting was what the gun lobby wanted, no press people, no hangers-on, just the two main protagonists, John and Linda, with two legal advisers each. It was to take place in a conference room in an undisclosed office building in Washington, DC.

Linda and her team arrived at the conference room first. She was wearing a dark-blue suit over a white-laced blouse, which complemented her dark-brown skin. She looked more like a lawyer than a nurse. She had taken the time to put on some make-up and polish her plain nails. She knew this was the moment of a significant confrontation. All her advocacy efforts in the past year had been building up to this moment. She could not help but be anxious despite assurances from her talented legal team that they could handle her adversary. Both lawyers were gun-control advocates just like her, and both had lost a loved one due to gun violence. They were confident. They were ready for John B. Cassfield.

John B. Cassfield walked in with his two advisers. They were smiling at each other as they found their seats from across Linda's team, but they quickly got serious as they sat down. A female stenographer sat at one end of the table. Cassfield spoke first.

"Mrs. Linda Santos, my name is John B. Cassfield," he said and extended his hand for a handshake. Linda responded by reaching out to shake his hand too. "First of all, you can call me John. I hope you will agree to let us call you Linda. Is that okay?"

"Okay," Linda agreed.

"Linda, I think there is a big divide in the way each of us understands the gun issue. Our goal to-day is to be able to narrow that divide and help pass sensible laws that will govern the gun industry. Do you agree, Linda?"

"Yes." He was smooth. Linda was impressed.

"Okay, regarding the issue of background checks—" Cassfield began.

Linda suddenly interrupted while Cassfield was in midsentence. "You are living by the gun, Mr. Cassfield," Linda said in a louder tone of voice, her face twitching in anger.

"Excuse me, Linda, I'd like to finish what I have to say before you speak, ma'am." Cassfield was obvi-ously irritated at the sudden interruption. He paused for a few seconds and then continued. "As I was saying, background checks are never effective—"

"You are living by the gun, John, as you know quite well, guarantees that you will die by the gun!" Linda again interrupted, her face showing the contortions of a vengeful advocate for innocent dead juveniles.

"Excuse me, Mrs. Santos!" John B. Cassfield stood up and raised his voice. "Could we please have some order in this meeting?"

"Mr. John B. Cassfield. As long as guns are being sold unregulated in your loophole states, the souls of my juvenile gun victims will never be at peace!" Linda spoke with fiery anger in her eyes. All her frustrations were coming out in her every sentence.

"But, Mrs. Santos, that's the reason why we're here, to come up with the best way to make sensible gun laws!" one of Cassfield's attorneys said, trying to reason with Linda.

"There is no compromise, Mr. Attorney. Children are being shot every day; just come to our emergency room, and their voices deserve to be heard."

Cassfield and his team stood up to leave, unable to shut Linda up. But Linda was not finished. This time she looked straight into Cassfield's eyes.

"John, there is a bullet out there with your name engraved on it, and it could hit you any time." Cassfield and his team started to walk out. Linda continued to speak.

"It could hit you, John, the moment you walk out that door!" Linda shouted. Those were her parting words to Cassfield, whose team opened the door and determinedly walked out.

Linda heaved a sigh of relief as she sat in her chair again. She had tears in her eyes from letting out the frustration she had felt for a long time. Her two lawyers were stunned at what she'd done.

One of them said, "I can't understand you, Linda. Why did you do that when we'd come so close to achieving our gun regulations?"

"Yes, Linda, wasn't this the compromise we've all worked so hard for?" The other attorney agreed.

Confident that she knew what she was doing, Linda said, "The meeting is not over yet." She wiped the tears from her cheeks with a tissue that smudged her light makeup. Then she opened her handbag, looking for something inside it. The three of them waited patiently for about ten minutes

Sure enough, one of Cassfield's attorneys came back to the room wanting to speak to Linda's attorneys. The three attorneys spoke to each other in muffled tones in one corner of the room. Linda could hear their low voices and see them all nodding their heads in some form of agreement. Then her attorneys came back to the table to talk to Linda.

"Cassfield wants to come back and resume the meeting," they reported to Linda.

She smiled confidently and replied, "Olay, please call them back."

Cassfield and his attorneys came back. Their faces looked so defeated and humiliated by the act of coming back. Now it was Linda's turn to speak.

"I'm sorry, John, if I was out of control. What I was doing was speaking on behalf of the children. They did not have a chance to argue and compromise the way we are doing now."

"But Linda…"

"With all due respect, John, let the dead speak through me first, and then I'll allow you to speak all you want. Can we do that, John?" Cassfield nodded in partial surrender. Everyone calmed down and waited for Linda to speak.

"I want to report to you, John, that I bought a gun." Linda paused to take a deep breath. "I bought the gun on the street for seventy-five dollars. It's a Glock G43 revolver. It was cheap and easy." She'd gotten their attention. "Let me tell you, John, when I held that gun, I felt so empowered that I wanted to shoot my neighbor's barking dog. Are you familiar with a Glock G43, John?" Linda opened her handbag and brought out the bullet that had been removed from her shoulder. "This is a bullet from a Glock G43, the one taken from my shoulder when I was shot." Linda held the bullet up with her right hand to show everyone in the room. "If I had died from that bullet, John, I would have been a meaningless, insignificant statistic to you and your gun people." Linda stood up and bent over to look closer at Cassfield. "People are standing up against you and your gun fanatics, John. You can no longer ignore our pain, our despair, and our numbers." Then she looked at Cassfield's two lawyers. "One day soon, you too will feel the pain of that bullet that tore through my flesh," she said. Her face was red with anger.

"How did you get that bullet past security?" one of Cassfield's attorneys asked.

"I am a crazy woman, Mr. Attorney! When your people shot at my family, you terrified my children. Their house is where they are supposed to feel the safest. And that made me a crazy woman. When you shot at my family, I became a vengeful, crazy mother. You have no idea!"

"But those were not my people, Linda. They were acting on their own."

"That could be, John, but if your gun people start shooting at law-abiding people, what that means is you don't want to compromise. You just want to prove to all of us that keeping your guns is all that matters to you and that those children's lives meant nothing at all to you." Linda's angry eyes were fixed on John, who seemed to feel that discomfort.

"Again, Linda, I don't know them, and I don't know what those people were thinking."

"That means that you cannot control those gun thugs, John, and that one day they will point their guns at you."

Yielding to a short, brown-skinned female might not be a winning negotiation score, but the inevitable concession from the gun lobby would have to come at some time. Too many innocent lives had been cut short so abruptly, without any warning. Children who were just starting to be aware of the realities of the world around them and just beginning to give hints of their promise were now senselessly gone. Thankfully, there was this Waray, this caring nurse who felt the need to speak for them and make sure those gun-crazy people understood.

The two parties hammered out the details. Sensible gun-control regulations through congressional legislation would be endorsed by the gun lobby, both parties agreed. The two groups shook hands with each other in respectful agreement. John B. Cassfield's team left the room first. Linda turned to the stenographer.

"Did you record everything that happened here?" she asked.

"Yes, ma'am. I also noted that the other party walked out and came back and that they were moved by the bullet you showed them." She paused and then asked Linda a question. "Tell me again, Mrs. Santos, how did you get your bullet past security?"

"Two of the guards were my previous patients."
She smiled. "I told them this was the only way to confront those cowardly gun people, by aiming a bullet
at them."

REVIEWS

"Gene has done a great job of entertaining us with his wonderful short stories; once you start reading, you don't want to stop. Very addicting!" **Eduardo Flor**

"This book is an inspirational collection of stories that view life's every day experiences with insightful storylines and good morals." **Mary Esther P. Wyman**

"The author, Gene P. Del Carmen, is a gifted writer who is able to inject moral lessons in all the stories. There is always a take-home message that speaks to our souls. It's refreshing to read stories of this kind especially in this tumultuous social climate." **Agnes T. Monta**

"Reading Gene P. Del Carmen's easy narratives is never a task at all. It's like having your favorite dessert—always a

nice treat, always a pleasure. I look forward to reading his stories all the time." **Lourdes C. Paredes**

"So far I have enjoyed all the short stories, stories I would have written myself had I known how." **Rogie Sanchez**

ABOUT THE AUTHOR

Gene P. Del Carmen has written short stories for illustrated comics and television scripts in Manila. He now works as a corporate accountant in New Jersey, where he also lives with his wife Arielita. He recently graduated with an MA in theology. This is his second book.